MW01138583

MYSTERY, SNOW, AND MISTLETOE

SWEETFERN HARBOR MYSTERY #6

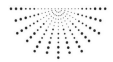

WENDY MEADOWS

Copyright © 2017 by Wendy Meadows

All rights reserved.

No part of this publication may be reproduced, distributed or
transmitted in any form or by any means, without prior written
permission.

This is a work of fiction. Names, characters, places, and incidents are a
product of the author's imagination. Locales and public names are
sometimes used for atmospheric purposes. Any resemblance to actual
people, living or dead, or to businesses, companies, events, institutions,
or locales is completely coincidental.

Printed in the United States of America

CHAPTER ONE

WISHES AND DREAMS

*B*renda Sheffield watched the plentiful snowflakes fall to the ground. The blanket of snow lay softly on the front lawn of Sheffield Bed and Breakfast in a pristine panorama. Early December was at last graced with beauty. Phyllis Lindsey stood beside Brenda, the owner of the bed and breakfast, and took in the beauty.

"I hope the day of our weddings looks like this, don't you, Brenda?"

"It would make a lovely day for sure."

The housekeeper and her boss planned to marry the loves of their lives in a double ceremony on Christmas Eve. Both anticipated the big day just like young brides-to-be would, even though they were both well past their twenties. Age didn't mar their excitement. In fact, the entire atmosphere of the bed and breakfast was revved up and animated at the prospect of the upcoming celebrations.

"I'm going to make some hot chocolate," Brenda said. "If you will find Allie, the three of us can start sorting through the Christmas decorations. I'm glad we finally got the Thanksgiving and fall décor put away until next year. Now we just have to sort through the enormous amount of Christmas stuff."

Brenda left for the kitchen while Phyllis located Allie, the young reservationist. A short time later, the three of them settled comfortably in chairs in the sitting room, where a fire crackled in the fireplace and made the room seem cozy in contrast to the snow-covered landscape outside. Brenda was reminded of the many times in the past when she and her mother sipped hot chocolate on cold winter days in Michigan. Her mother always made sure they greeted her truck-driver father with steaming hot chocolate when he came home in cold weather. Tim Sheffield always protested that he preferred coffee, but he willingly accepted the sweet, hot beverage without complaint, every time.

"There are still the four large Christmas trees down in storage," Allie said. "Do you want me to ask Michael to bring them up?"

"I don't think so. Allie, I've been thinking...there is

2

something about those pre-lit, artificial trees that just doesn't appeal to me. It doesn't feel right. This year we are going to have the real thing." Allie grinned happily to hear this and Phyllis smiled as she took another sip of her hot chocolate. Brenda had thought the plan through a little, and shared it with them. "We'll take the truck and go to that huge tree farm at the edge of town and pick out perfect trees."

The other women agreed with excitement. "I love the smell of real evergreens," Allie said. "My mother won't have anything but the real thing at home, or even in her bakery, Sweet Treats."

"Just the mention of those delectable sweets of hers makes my mouth water," Phyllis said. "Hope Williams is the best when it comes to baking."

Brenda hopped up and went back into the kitchen. Her mouth curved from ear to ear when she came back. "Hope just sent these muffins over. She's testing special new Christmas recipes – that one is cranberry walnut, this one is gingerbread with candied oranges. And I think this one is eggnog spice! Try one." No more encouragement was needed, and everyone quickly selected a treat to try.

"All right now," Brenda said. "Let's start digging into these boxes. This afternoon we will go tree-hunting."

After a couple of hours, the decorations were decided.

They had unearthed some beautiful antique treasures that had been collected by her uncle during his ownership of the bed and breakfast, as well as newer ones that had been gifts from guests, or bought at local craft fairs. Brenda refilled their cups of hot chocolate and then opened the door to the wide covered porch.

She sighed. "I loved the snows in Michigan, but there is something really special about a New England snowfall."

Phyllis pulled her tweed sweater tighter. She had grown up in Sweetfern Harbor and she still thought the same about this part of the country. Every season displayed its own beauty and she savored nature – almost as much as she did William Pendleton, the man of her dreams. Brenda noticed her sudden pensive change. Phyllis's eyes appeared far away. Brenda moved closer to her friend.

"What is it, Phyllis? I can tell something is bothering you."

"My aunt who raised me often told me that when the first snowfall hit Sweetfern Harbor, it meant that all of my dreams and wishes of the season would come true."

"William is your dream come true," Brenda said. She couldn't imagine Phyllis having any doubts.

"He is my stalwart," she said with a fond smile. "I have no doubts about him at all. I love him so much." She gazed at the still-whitening landscape. "But I do have one more wish for my wedding day. It's my brother, Patrick. I wish I knew where he was so I could get him here."

"You've only spoken of him once that I recall, when you asked me if I had siblings. I always meant to ask you... what happened to Patrick? I mean, do you have any idea why he went off somewhere?"

Phyllis shook her head. "He disappeared suddenly, five years ago. Edward Graham employed him as a clerk at his law office and Patrick seemed very happy with his job. He loved learning all he could about the justice system and Edward took him on as an apprentice of sorts. Patrick always wanted to get a law degree, though he was in his early fifties already."

"Did he live by himself, or was he married?"

Phyllis's laugh was a quick one. "He could have had anyone he wanted. His personality could win any woman over." She paused, her warm memories coming to mind. "He really had a great sense of humor, too. He lived alone and had an apartment downtown." Her hand flew to her mouth and her eyes widened. "Oh, dear. I vowed to never use the past tense when talking about him, or thinking about him. I am sure he is still alive and out there somewhere. I just wish he would contact me."

Brenda put a sympathetic arm around her dear friend's shoulders. She couldn't help but start thinking like a sleuth, however. "Did the police have any leads on his whereabouts?"

"Both Chief Ingram and your Detective Mac Rivers spent a lot of time on the case after I reported him missing. But they always came up with dead ends. Someone must know where he is." Phyllis's eyes lit up. "You are good at detective work, Brenda. Maybe you could meet with Bob and Mac and see something they didn't see. Nothing would make me happier than to have my brother at my wedding."

Brenda paused, touched by the intense feeling evident in her friend's eyes. Decorating the bed and breakfast for the holidays, preparing for the double wedding and looking into a missing person case sounded like a crowded agenda, but Brenda knew she had no choice. She squeezed Phyllis's hands and vowed to do everything she could to find Phyllis her most desired wedding present. "I'll talk with the chief and Mac. As soon as I can, Phyllis. But in the meantime, let's grab some lunch and then head out to cut down a tree."

Phyllis wiped a tear of relief away at Brenda's promise, but then laughed. "You don't have to cut it down, you know. They're all pre-cut, unless you want to find one out in the tree lot. Even then, they'll go chop it down for you." Phyllis's demeanor lightened. Brenda was glad to see her friend in jovial spirits again.

"That's good," Brenda said. "I'm not sure I'd cut the tree

down without cutting off a piece of my body, with my luck." They laughed and headed back into the bed and breakfast.

In the front hall, they found Allie talking to a guest. She told the young woman that lunch was ready and offered to walk with them to the dining room.

"We'll all go together," Brenda said.

In the dining room, everyone was abuzz about the snowfall and more than one guest remarked about the exquisite views outside. "I don't want to walk down to the seawall," one said. "It will mess up the smooth blanket of snow."

It was unusual for them to still have this many guests at the bed and breakfast so close to Christmas. Most years, Sheffield Bed and Breakfast became quieter and quieter as the winter season closed in and then closed down completely for Christmastime. But this year would be different. There were two sets of brides and grooms who planned to marry and then take off on their honeymoons. This year, the bed and breakfast would close for almost two weeks to prepare and make everything as beautiful and festive as possible.

After the lunch, they headed out to the truck. Brenda thought about how much she looked forward to spending her honeymoon with Mac in Italy. Phyllis and William planned to go to St. Thomas in the U.S. Virgin Islands.

They liked the warm temperatures and the deep blue ocean. Phyllis had told Brenda that William loved snorkeling and he wanted to teach her how to explore the life beneath the sea. Brenda had been surprised at first, but then realized her housekeeper really looked forward to any experience with William Pendleton.

They soon arrived at the Christmas tree farm on their quest for the perfect trees.

"I wonder how many acres there are here," Brenda said in wonder as she stepped out of the truck and gazed around. "It will be hard to choose even one." Across the tree farm, the snowy branches of beautiful, perfect evergreens were outlined with snow. A large log cabin building held the main offices of the farm, where visitors could stop by and warm up on their way in or out. Wood smoke rose invitingly into the chilly air from its stone chimney.

A young man appeared behind them with a friendly greeting, having overheard Brenda. "Welcome! We have fifty acres total. If you can't find a pre-cut one I'll take you out and we'll find one for you."

"We want four trees, maybe five." Brenda caught herself before she got too carried away. She had to remember the wedding coming up. Things were expensive enough.

Phyllis and Allie stared at her and then smiled. Phyllis knew she would have to rein in her boss, but not yet. "Let's get started," she said.

"I think we shouldn't waste time looking at pre-cut ones. Let's go out and cut our own." Allie's eyes sparkled. "I mean he said he would cut it if we found ours."

The young man introduced himself as Jason. He had worked there for a couple years and knew the trees well. He suggested a particular field that held a number of beautiful trees they might find just right. All agreed to ride out with Jason and pick their own.

"There is no way I can choose," Brenda repeated. The truck stopped so they could get out and start their search. Phyllis and Allie climbed out from the second-row seat behind Brenda and Jason.

"Let's start with the Frasier Firs," Jason said. He pointed out the attributes of the fir and asked how tall of a tree they wanted.

"The ceilings of the bed and breakfast are ten feet tall, some higher." Brenda looked at Phyllis for direction.

"Let's look at six or eight-foot trees, then." Jason had taken over decision-making. He confidently pointed out the pros and cons of several trees they were drawn to. Allie skipped ahead of them in her snow boots and pointed to a magnificent fir tree. There were no bare spots to be seen.

"This is our first one," she said.

Jason tested the Frasier Fir that Allie had picked out for

any dryness. The seven-foot tree was healthy. They agreed he could bring it down and he made quick work of it with a chainsaw. Allie helped him load it onto the open-bed trailer. By this time, Brenda had a better idea of what to look for. She remembered that back in Michigan, her father always picked out pine trees for Christmas.

"Do you have any pines?" she asked, looking around. Jason grinned and nodded.

They all climbed back into the truck and headed for the White Pines. After another hour, everyone was satisfied with the two Frasier Firs and two White Pines they had cut fresh. When they got back to the parking lot, Jason directed them to the large log building, telling them to go inside and sip some hot cider or chocolate while he prepared their trees for transportation and tied them securely to the bed of their truck.

Once inside, Brenda couldn't get enough of the evergreen scent that permeated the air. They all seemed to carry it with them on their coats like a perfume after walking through the fields of trees. The hot chocolate not only tasted good, but warmed them up.

"I think we should get some evergreen branches, too. You could make some beautiful wreaths, Allie, with your artistic talent," Brenda commented. She was looking at the fireplace nearby, which held a few fir swags and festive ribbon, picturing what that might look like at the Sheffield.

Phyllis was tempted to remind Brenda of the budget. She knew Brenda stuck by it no matter what. She knew Brenda was still paying off the mortgage on the bed and breakfast, which she had inherited from her uncle. Phyllis could not help but enjoy the expression of contentment on her friend's face, so she decided against spoiling things. After all, everything Brenda picked out would also serve as décor for the double wedding reception, which would take place at Sheffield Bed and Breakfast following the double wedding ceremony at the Congregational Church. It was a mark of their deep and lasting friendship that Phyllis and Brenda were so committed to the idea of everything coming together for their perfect double wedding on Christmas Eve.

When they finished their hot cocoa and headed back outside, Jason had loaded the trees into Brenda's truck. She handed him a generous tip for his work and they all climbed in. They sang Christmas carols all the way home and waved to everyone they knew as they passed the specialty shops along the main street, each one more festive than the last. The town was decorated to the point where it truly looked like a Christmas wonderland.

Happiness soared through Brenda's heart as they pulled up to Sheffield House and once again she thanked her uncle, Randolph Sheffield, for his generosity to her in his will. Without him, she would not be the owner of the bed and breakfast, which meant she wouldn't be riding down the street with four Christmas trees in the back of a truck with two good friends, looking ahead to marrying the man of her dreams.

Never in her wildest dreams did she think she would ever live in a place like Sweetfern Harbor. In all of New England, Brenda couldn't imagine there was a happier, more perfect place for the Christmas season ahead.

CHAPTER TWO

KEEPING PROMISES

Tim Sheffield looked out his window from the second floor of the 1890 Queen Anne Victorian mansion. He shook his head and laughed softly when he saw his daughter Brenda alight from the well-worn pickup truck. He would have gone with the women to find the perfect tree, but he had business that morning with his accountant back in Michigan. The phone call had taken even longer than he'd first hoped, but at last he was satisfied everything was in order. He took a second look at the truck in the driveway. Brenda had gone a little wild, he thought. He hurried into his winter jacket and pulled his thick woolen cap onto his head and went downstairs and out the door.

"What all did you buy at that tree farm?" he asked. "It

looks like you didn't leave anything for other people who may want a tree or two."

Brenda took his teasing in stride. She was more than happy her father had decided to stay through the holidays. More than that, she was grateful they had mended the rift between them that had seemed so impossibly wide when he first arrived at Thanksgiving. After all they had been through, there was no animosity left between them.

"Come on and lend a hand," she told her dad. "We could use some help here."

Several employees hurried out to help. They were eager to get started on the decorating and had the tree stands ready for each tree that came off the truck. It took two or three people to carry each tree inside and set them up throughout the bed and breakfast. Brenda stood next to her father when they finished.

"Have you ever seen such tall trees?" she asked him.

"I haven't, unless you are counting what's out in the forests." He gave a grunt of satisfaction, looking up at the tallest tree posed in the window. "You three did a good job picking these out." Brenda hid a smile. Tim Sheffield was a man of few words, so this was high praise.

She and Tim left the group to their tasks. Allie had already started carrying armfuls of fir branches from the truck to the large utility shed behind the bed and breakfast. William had helped set up a long work table and donated a box of supplies for wreath making, saying that Allie Williams needed the right tools if she was to develop her creative talents. The teenager was elated and immediately set to work.

Brenda and her father settled in her apartment. He poured himself a cup of coffee and she opted for a cup of hot raspberry tea. They talked of Christmases past and chuckled over their shared memories. There was a soft knock on her door and she opened it to find Mac leaning on the doorframe with a slow smile, only for her. There was never even one time that her heart didn't do a flip-flop when she saw him. She invited him in and he accepted a cup of coffee.

"I don't want to interfere with your visit," he said, waving hello to Tim.

Tim waved Mac's excuses away. "We see each other every day. I just made Brenda bring me up here to get out of all the work." They laughed at his humor and settled in.

"Well, you're in luck, they're mostly done. I think I only saw one tree downstairs that wasn't finished," Mac said. "I take it that's not for Tim to decorate?" He laughed. "I already heard about your wild trip to the Christmas tree farm. You did a great job on choosing the right trees. I think Phyllis said the White Pine was your favorite? I believe they left that one for you, Brenda."

She smiled, touched. "I do love decorating...I guess I was bushed when we got back. Let's go down and see what's left to do."

All three went downstairs. "We left the tree in the dining room for you to do, Brenda. I know you really liked the White Pine." Phyllis waited for her response.

"I'm ready to get busy. I have help so we'll start now. I want it finished by dinnertime tonight."

Brenda thanked the others for their hard work and told them all to take a break. The Sheffield Bed and Breakfast had transformed into a Christmas vision, with lights and decorations on the trees artfully posed in the windows of the main rooms.

Mac, her father and Brenda all went into the large dining room. The tree was in the middle of the bay window that looked out onto the snowy side lawn, across which one could see the ocean. The bed and breakfast was on a slight promontory and so Brenda realized that perhaps ships passing in the night would get a glimpse of the lit tree. The tree had been carefully draped with lights, and a box of ornaments set to one side for her to select from. But she did not want to look in the box just yet. Instead, Brenda pulled a small ornament from her pocket and carefully hung it from a branch so it caught the light just so. It was a perfect, tiny replica of the bed and breakfast, painted exactly as in real life, down to the smallest detail.

"Where did you get that?" Tim asked.

"I made it," Brenda said with pride. "I've been secretly taking craft classes downtown. I had to prove I can do something when I'm surrounded by so much talent."

Mac hugged her and admired the ornament for a moment, then pulled a box from his pocket. "I brought something you might like to add to the tree." A crystal ornament glittered in the box, and it was engraved with their names. Brenda gasped. She told him it was beautiful and happily hung the first ornament they shared together.

They decorated the rest of the pine until finished. "Let's not forget the tree lighting ceremony downtown tonight," Mac said. "Do you want to come with us, Tim?"

"I'll pass on that. I've got enough to enjoy right here, and besides, you two should have some time together to enjoy the holiday."

He watched his forty-six-year-old daughter grin and blush like a schoolgirl as her fiancé held her tightly to his side. It seemed that was always her mood when she was with the detective. Tim thought about his deceased wife and wished she could be here now to see where their daughter's life had taken her.

"It's much colder than it was earlier, Brenda. Bundle up." Mac assisted her into her woolen coat. The Sherpa lining ensured warmth as they walked toward the park through the chilly December evening. "We're a little early...let's stop at Molly's for some hot coffee," Mac suggested, seeing the inviting glow of the coffee shop's windows ahead.

Phyllis's daughter Molly Lindsey had made a success of Morning Sun Coffee. She had even hired two more employees during the fall to help with the holiday season and they still kept busy enough. Brenda and Mac moved through the crowd and found a table in the corner of the shop. Most customers stood in line to order take-out beverages and sandwiches.

Brenda shrugged her coat off her shoulders and Mac draped it over the empty chair next to her. He sat across from her. Brenda looked around and then her eyes stopped. She stared at something with such consternation that it caused Mac to turn around and try to see what it was.

"Do you see the same thing I'm seeing?" she asked in an undertone.

Young Detective Bryce Jones, Mac's colleague and the boyfriend of Mac's daughter Jenny, leaned toward Molly at the front counter. Molly laughed and tried to brush him off while she took orders. Something told Brenda that Molly's efforts were not sincere. As she watched, it seemed as if Molly was enjoying the attention. Bryce was known to be a terrible flirt, but Brenda thought that Jenny Rivers had cured him of that habit long ago.

"What's there to see? Bryce is still a big flirt," Mac said. "I do worry about Jenny sometimes."

Brenda knew Mac cherished his daughter and hovered over her like a mother hen at times, but this time she thought he may have a real reason to worry. She watched the pair closely. Just then, Molly called an employee to take her place. She and Bryce moved to the end of the counter to talk. Their conversation couldn't be heard by Brenda and Mac but their mannerisms clearly indicated that something was going on between the two of them. Molly turned when someone gave her the tray of hot drinks. She said something to Bryce and headed toward Brenda and Mac.

"I think you ordered the peppermint coffee, Brenda, and the eggnog coffee for you, Mac." She asked if they planned to go to the tree lighting. Brenda was flustered and did not reply, looking down at her coffee and taking a big sip. When Mac replied yes, Molly glanced back at Bryce, who stood in the same spot. "Bryce and I are going too, as soon as I can get away from here."

Mac frowned. "Is Jenny sick? I don't see her in here and it looked like she may have closed Blossoms already."

Molly's eyes opened wide. "I guess you haven't heard. As far as I know, Jenny is fine. She and Pete Graham are meeting us here."

"What is it that we haven't heard?" Brenda asked in confusion.

At that moment, Jenny's melodious laugh could be heard above the sounds of the café, and they turned to see Jenny and Pete walking toward their table.

"What's going on here?" Mac asked, his brow furrowed with concern as his daughter arrived.

"We'll get some coffee and join you soon. Don't leave," Jenny said, ducking his question. She and Pete went back to the counter and got in line.

"I'm sorry, Mac, I thought Jenny would have told you... Bryce started paying a lot more attention to me than Pete ever has. He is hard to resist. It turned out that Pete has liked Jenny for a long time and we had a long talk. We decided to allow me to date Bryce and Pete is free to date Jenny. It's worked out very well and we're all happy. We're giving it all a try, anyway."

The news was startling. Flashbacks of the summer when an acting troupe arrived in Sweetfern Harbor to perform "The Rich Game" sent waves of bad memories through Brenda. The play was a comedy about couples who switched partners, but the outcome in real life had not been pleasant. The star of the show was found dead in the Sheffield Bed and Breakfast. She hoped this would end better.

Mac simmered inside. His face had flushed, listening to

Molly's explanation. He was aware that the young detective felt a compulsion to flirt with a different girl every month or so. He had warned his daughter about Bryce's wayward eyes and she had laughed at him, assuring him she knew how to keep him in line. They had dated for months without any incident, in fact. Mac thought about Pete Graham, the mailman. Pete was the son of the town lawyer. He gossiped along his route to the point where everyone eagerly awaited the latest news from him when he brought their mail. Mac wasn't sure what to think about Jenny dating Pete.

Jenny returned just then and set her coffee down, and Pete took the second empty chair.

"I'm ready to tell you what's going on," Jenny started to explain.

"Never mind," Mac said, "Molly already told us." He locked eyes with his daughter. Mixed feelings churned through him – relief that Bryce was no longer a worry, but also concern about Pete dating his daughter. It all caused Mac to push away his half-empty cup of eggnog coffee. Pete was all right, but not the one for his Jenny. There was a short, uncomfortable silence as everyone sipped their coffee. Mac cleared his throat and tried again. "We'll talk later at home, Jenny. We haven't had a lot of time to talk about anything lately, what with all the holiday festivities."

Brenda took over for Mac and commented that they were

going down to the park for the tree lighting. Mac was silent, but Jenny would not let him retreat, and said she would see him there. Her crystal blue eyes danced in the soft glow of the lamps in the coffee shop.

Later, Brenda curled her arm through Mac's as they set off down the sidewalk toward the park. He was still upset. "This is the kind of thing Jenny needs her mother for," Mac said. The cold wind whipped their faces. "I had no idea this was going on."

"I don't think anyone could guide her right now, Mac. It seems this all just started. It will probably blow over when they realize who is really meant for whom." She picked up her pace to match his and hoped the mood of the evening would change.

Mac pulled her closer to his side, grateful for her softness and her optimism, even when his own heart was clouded with worry.

They heard the Christmas carols when they were still a block away from the park. Large crowds had begun to gather and they saw Hope Williams's bakery truck pull up. David and Hope got out and carried large trays of sweets to a long table set up near the carolers. As they drew closer, Brenda noticed a variety of cookies, each tray a particular flavor decorated to match the holiday spirit. They greeted the owner of Sweet Treats. Allie arrived and also helped her parents unload the last of the goodies.

"I hope this is enough," Hope said, stepping back to admire her handiwork. The icing on some of the cookies practically sparkled.

"If you run out, it will make even more people want to come into Sweet Treats and buy some," David joked. "Mac, Brenda, help yourself."

His words and buoyant spirit were a godsend and lifted Mac and Brenda's moods. They each took a cookie and then found a spot to wait for the tree lighting.

"That spruce is beautiful," Brenda said. "Look how tall it is."

"I'd say it has to be close to twenty feet," Mac said. "The town outdid itself this year."

"I'm sure William Pendleton had something to do with it."

Brenda was happy for Phyllis. Marrying William would complete her life. Having her brother Patrick home again would be the icing on the cake for Phyllis. They listened to the singers as more people gathered. Molly closed her shop earlier than expected since her workers also wanted to enjoy the lighting. She, Bryce, Jenny and Pete joined Brenda and Mac. For now, Mac chose to ignore the foursome's strange new configuration. Instead, he greeted them and simply commented on the tree and the carolers.

It wasn't long before the music director, Mr. Hale,

finished conducting the carolers' song and turned to the crowd. He invited everyone to sing along for the remaining songs.

Brenda and Mac sang along and Mac's baritone voice captured Brenda more than the carols did. When the singing stopped, Mr. Hale held up his hand and introduced William.

"William Pendleton, who graciously sponsored this wonderful event, will give the signal for the tree lighting shortly. In the meantime, enjoy the refreshments and company around you. We will sing more carols after the lighting."

Everyone clapped and cheered loudly. Brenda had an idea.

"I think we should have the high school choir sing at our wedding. They are really good."

Mac agreed. "Let's find Reverend Walker. I saw him a while ago. I don't think he would mind."

When they saw the minister who would be marrying them, they waved at him. He smiled back and greeted them. Brenda asked him about the idea of the choir singing at the wedding. He agreed right away.

"It's your wedding. If you and the other couple want the choir to sing, it is fine with me. It would sound beautiful to have them sing along with the organ. They can sing from the choir loft."

Snow began falling again. William stood at the podium a few yards from the tree and announced it was time for the lighting. Everything was dark. Even the streetlights had been turned off around the park for the occasion. Then the tree lit up everything with its soft, bright glow and the crowd clapped and cheered again. The choir sang "O, Little Town of Bethlehem" followed by "Jingle Bells." The snowflakes that fell softly were now large enough that they could see each perfect shape as it fell, and Mac bent and kissed Brenda's soft lips.

CHAPTER THREE

MYSTERIOUS DISAPPEARANCE

When Brenda got out of bed the next morning, the feelings of the night before awakened within her. Christmastime in Sweetfern Harbor was magical. The sparkling expanse of the snowy lawn outside greeted her when she looked out the window. Meanwhile, the busy Sheffield Bed and Breakfast began to wind down for the season. This was the time for Brenda and all her employees to enjoy the season.

Brenda remembered that today was the day that she and Allie planned to go Christmas shopping together. Last night when they had spoken about it, Allie told her mother Hope that she needed to go shopping with Brenda just for one day, since she wanted to find the perfect gift for her mother without spoiling the surprise.

Hope had smiled and made her promise to finish shopping with her later, as was their custom. Brenda smiled to remember how David Williams sighed audibly, hefting another tray of delectable sweets onto the table at the tree lighting, as his wife and daughter laughed at him. David knew the ritual and had stopped chiding them for bringing home "everything from every store."

Brenda downed the last sip of her coffee and joined Allie, who was already in the front hall. Together, bundled up in their warmest jackets, they walked past the frozen pond and waved to the children and a few adults skating on it.

"I'd like to start with gift-buying for my bridesmaids," Brenda said. She had chosen Jenny, Molly, Allie and Hope for that role. "I hope you have some good ideas for me, Allie. Just remember, each gift has to be different."

There was something Allie knew how to do better than anyone, and that was shopping. She grinned fiercely at Brenda, ready for the challenge. "Have you picked out your wedding cake?" Allie asked as their footsteps crunched along in the snow.

"I haven't forgotten that. Today is as good a day as ever. Let's stop at your mother's shop and indulge in some tasting before we hit the stores." Allie was delighted and they quickly reached Sweet Treats.

As they entered, their mouths watered at the scent of

freshly-baked bagels of every flavor that Hope slid into glass display cases. "Brenda, Allie, what a surprise. How can I help you?" Allie told her mother that Brenda wanted to pick out her wedding cake.

"I know I didn't make an appointment," Brenda said apologetically, "so if this isn't a good time, I'll come back later."

Hope waved her words aside and called for an employee to take her place at the front counter. She led Allie and Brenda to the back. "You have good timing. I made up a few samples earlier this morning and was going to call you in for tasting." It seemed everyone in town was a step ahead of Brenda when it came to wedding planning. "I have a sample of a white butter cake and several others, including a spice flavor, if you want something more like gingerbread for the season." Brenda and Allie happily sat down with Hope at the baking table in the kitchen and each tried bites of the miniature frosted cakes. Each was delectable in its own way.

"They're all so delicious, Hope! It's impossible to decide. Let me try the second one again..." Brenda took another delicate forkful of the red velvet cake, which seemed to melt on her tongue. She remembered that Mac had mentioned liking red velvet cake, too. She smiled and nodded. "This is the one."

Hope said, "I hoped you would pick that one. If you want me to, I'll decorate it with holly leaves – edible, of course.

A few red berries will complete the festive look and it will be shaped like a traditional wedding cake." She sketched a picture for her, showing the five tiers of the cake with the decorations, and Brenda agreed readily. "Will Phyllis have a separate cake?" Hope asked.

"Phyllis and I decided to share the cake the way we are sharing our wedding day. She and I agreed on two flavors and one was red velvet, actually. I'll let her know it's in the works."

Brenda noticed Hope's hesitation as they stood up to go and asked her if she needed more from her. "I know you and Allie planned to go shopping, but we're swamped in here. Can you spare her for a couple of hours?"

"That will be fine, if Allie is agreeable. We don't have a full house at the bed and breakfast anyway. We can shop together later this evening or tomorrow." Allie agreed and gave her several suggestions for her bridesmaids' gifts.

Brenda thanked her and left them discussing imminent orders to be filled at Sweet Treats. It sounded like Allie and her mother had a full schedule of baking ahead of them. She had other things on her mind aside from shopping, however, and her steps headed for the Parsonage.

She hadn't forgotten about Phyllis's brother who mysteriously disappeared. Reverend Walker had lived and pastored in Sweetfern Harbor for the past twenty-five years. He surely knew Patrick Lindsey. Although she knew she needed to check in with Mac and the police chief about their cold case file on Phyllis's brother too, something made her want to get the human side of the story, first. When she rang the doorbell outside the beautifully carved front door of the Parsonage, Reverend Walker greeted her and invited her inside.

He ushered her into his study, a cozy wood-paneled room warmed by the crackling fire burning in the hearth and scented by the pine boughs of a handsome Christmas wreath that hung over the mantle. "Phyllis stopped by yesterday and added a few things to her wedding vows. Are you here for the same reason?"

Brenda was momentarily taken aback. "There is so much to think about when it comes to this wedding," she replied. "I had no idea so much was involved. But of course, vows are uppermost...or, they should be..."

From her flustered manner, Reverend Walker intuited that she had none prepared. He smiled at her reassuringly. "My dear, not to worry. I have taken care of that for you. The words I have written just have to be approved. You can add to them, if you wish, as Phyllis did." He handed Brenda a sheet of paper from his desk and Brenda read them over.

"I couldn't have written any words more meaningful," she said. "Thank you, Reverend. I'm so grateful to you. But vows aside...I have something else to discuss with you. Phyllis told me that more than anything she wishes that her brother could be here for her wedding. Did you know Patrick?"

Reverend Walker invited her to sit down in a worn but comfortable armchair. "I knew him and Phyllis quite well. She mentioned him to me when she was here yesterday."

"Was he an easy man to get along with?" Brenda asked. "By that I mean, did anyone have anything against him to cause him to vanish?"

"Patrick was well-liked on the whole. His sister is driven by hard work and doesn't seem to let up, as you have found out. On the other hand, Patrick tended to be lazy, which led to somewhat of a careless attitude at times."

Brenda asked for clarification. Reverend Walker told her that Patrick riled some people with his outspokenness. "He spoke his thoughts before thinking about how the receiver would take his words. He didn't hold down jobs long, either. He was a pretty good worker as long as he liked what he was doing, but soon moved on."

Reverend Walker told her Patrick had worked in the local library for a while. She knew Mrs. Perch, the librarian, and made a mental note to visit with her. She jerked her head up when Reverend Walker mentioned Patrick had worked for Edward Graham, the town lawyer.

"Did he like working for him?"

The Reverend shrugged. "He seemed to like the field of law. In fact, he held onto that job longer than any other. It was the last job he had in town before he just disappeared. You might want to talk with Matthew Wilkins who owns the little grocery store in town. He liked Patrick and mentioned once how hard he worked stocking the shelves at night and other odd jobs there. It was a good job for him because his apartment was downtown near the grocer."

"Did he live in that apartment long?"

"I don't recall exactly, but long enough to think of him as always there. I don't remember him living anywhere else, since I came to know him, anyway."

Brenda thanked him for everything and headed back outside into the cold winter day. She glanced at her watch. She had time to grab a light lunch at Morning Sun Coffee and think things over. The more she learned about Patrick Lindsey, the more she wanted to help find him. She felt Phyllis's life would be complete if that happened. What better gift for her best friend and most loyal employee?

Molly greeted Brenda warmly when she came in. She wiped her hands on the edge of her apron and carried two hot drinks to Brenda's table. "I'm going to take a short break. I hope you don't mind if I join you."

Brenda invited her to sit down. "How well did you know your uncle?"

Molly grinned, she could tell when Brenda was working on a case. "Patrick Lindsey is my only uncle, so I know you are asking about him. I loved him. He was a lot of fun and always joked around with me a lot." Her eyes grew sad. "I wish we knew where he went. I always wondered if there was foul play of some kind. I just wish I knew what happened to him. My mother still grieves over the loss."

"It sounds as if you think he isn't alive."

"I don't want to think that, but why hasn't he come home?"

Brenda asked her if she had seen Patrick just before he vanished. Molly told her he had come into her shop, had his usual breakfast and chatted for a while. "He was happy," she said. "It was a Saturday in July. The sun was out and he mentioned how refreshing the sea breeze felt that morning. Your uncle was in here that morning, too. Randolph liked Patrick. They talked about the court case Patrick was fighting."

This shed new light on the subject. Brenda leaned in closer to Molly. "What was the court case about?"

"He had a case against Lady Pendleton. He was in great spirits, he told Randolph he had won the case. Lady Pendleton had raised his apartment rent to an exorbitant amount. He wasn't the only one, but he fought back. Edward Graham's good friend from nearby Oceanside took the case, because of course, Lady Pendleton retained Edward as her lawyer. Conflict of interest, you know."

Brenda nodded. She accepted a refill. A group of customers walked into the shop. Brenda wanted to find out more about Molly and Bryce, but that would have to wait. Molly excused herself and left to help with the sudden crowd.

Brenda walked back to her bed and breakfast to get her car. She called William Pendleton and asked if she could meet with him for a few minutes. He agreed and she left for his mansion.

William, as jovial as ever, invited her inside. A carafe of hot tea and one of hot coffee waited for her to decide. She chose the hot tea this time and reached for a thin slice of frosted pound cake. As they sat down to eat, she looked around and saw a number of wooden crates and cardboard boxes sitting around the room. She looked questioningly at William.

"I'm cleaning out today," he said. "As you can imagine, most of this stuff is meaningless to me. Priscilla was the collector, not me. So I am making room for the love of my life. Phyllis doesn't need to live around all of this stuff Priscilla seemed to cherish." He looked up from his cup of steaming coffee and smiled. "What brings you over to see me today?" She started to apologize for interrupting his task when he waved away her words, saying, "Please, it's a relief to get away from it all for a while. What do you need?"

If everyone didn't already know how tedious Lady Pendleton was during her marriage to William, terrorizing the townspeople with her outrageous and capricious demands for ever-increasing rents, Brenda would have felt nervous bringing up the subject. But she knew William would understand, especially if it was a matter dear to Phyllis's heart.

"I have been trying to trace Patrick Lindsey's whereabouts. Before Lady Pendleton passed away, Patrick Lindsey fought her in court over the matter of a rent increase. Molly told me she saw him the day before he disappeared – he was elated he won, and she had never seen him as happy as he was that Saturday morning when he came into the shop for breakfast. Something must have happened between that morning and the next one."

Brenda took a bite of her cake and then a sip of her tea, taking the opportunity to gather her courage before continuing. But luckily, William spoke first.

"And you are wondering if my late wife had anything to do with his disappearance." William waved his hand at her when she started to explain. "Don't think I haven't wondered about that myself, though I cannot recall anything that would point to her guilt. Priscilla wasn't an

easy woman, even though she had everything this world had to offer her. She was selfish and never satisfied. She certainly didn't enjoy losing a court battle. We all know that rarely happened. Edward Graham was her puppet in her despicable real estate dealings for many years, though I try to understand his position...he simply caved to her every wish to keep his position, and because he thought he could stop her from being even worse if she marched out of town and hired a big corporate law firm. She had immense power, as we all know."

Brenda nodded, thinking back to her brief encounters with Lady Priscilla with a shudder. "I promised Phyllis I would look into it. It would mean everything to her to have her brother back here for the wedding. She is so happy with you, William. I know your lives together will be wonderful."

She stood to go when the doorbell rang. Without waiting, Phyllis walked in. William kissed her lightly on the cheek. "What have I done to earn the presence of two such beautiful women at once?"

Phyllis laughed and told him he was lucky indeed. Brenda explained to her friend that she was investigating the disappearance of Patrick. Phyllis hugged her tightly and with tears in her eyes, she thanked Brenda.

"Those three boxes there have holiday decorations in them, Brenda," William said as she turned to go. "Priscilla bought them but they've never been used.

Some are fall decorations, and every other holiday you can think of. If you can use them, feel free to take them home with you." He summoned someone to help and the boxes were soon loaded into her car. "I know you will get to the bottom of this, Brenda," he said. "Let me know if I can be of any help. I have no clues right now, only some hunches. I don't like to think my late wife was a part of it, but we never know, do we?"

Brenda had climbed into her car and turned the key in the ignition when William approached her window. She opened the window, curious at the unreadable expression on his face. "You may want to look through those boxes before storing them. I know you are busy with Christmas and the wedding, but take a look inside them," he said, and then waved goodbye as he walked back to the shelter of the front door.

Brenda drove away, anxious to get home and delve into the boxes. She wondered what William hinted at and was sure something of great interest to her waited inside. When she arrived home, she drove around to the back of the bed and breakfast and noticed it seemed strange to see fewer cars parked in the guest spots. In the back, there were several employees' cars, and she parked next to them, planning to carry the boxes inside and inspect them right away. She couldn't get William's parting words out of her mind.

CHAPTER FOUR

MEMORIES

*T*here was a lot to think about in regard to Patrick Lindsey's disappearance. His lawyer must have been a good one to win over Lady Pendleton. From Lady Pendleton's fierce reputation and their few unfortunate encounters, Brenda understood how that wouldn't have sat well with her. She decided to pull into the garage behind the bed and breakfast, knowing there was more snow on the way and how much she disliked having to shovel her car out. Brenda walked through the back door of the bed and breakfast. She waved to Chef Morgan and went through the hallway that led to the front desk. A familiar, masculine voice reached her.

"You look pretty today, Allie." Bryce Jones leaned a little too close to Brenda's reservationist. The young girl blushed and looked up at her boss.

"What are you doing here, Bryce?" Brenda asked.

"I'm taking my break. I was hoping for some hot coffee for a hard-working detective."

"You are welcome to a cup of coffee in exchange for helping me unload some boxes from my car." Brenda turned and smiled to herself. She had the feeling Bryce didn't want to tear himself away from her pretty teenage employee.

Bryce winked at Allie and followed Brenda out to her car.

"What did you bring home this time?" he asked, hefting the first box from the trunk. She raised her eyebrows. "I mean, this one is heavy. Is there gold in it?"

"I wish," Brenda said. "It's just unused holiday decorations from the Pendleton home. William is cleaning out before Phyllis moves in with him, and offered them to me. I want to take them to my apartment so I can go through them before storing them away."

When the last box was set inside Brenda's door, Bryce asked Brenda if she had anything else that needed done. She told him she planned to bake some cookies and jokingly told him he was welcome to help her. To her surprise, he agreed enthusiastically.

"You look surprised, Brenda," he said with a chuckle, "but I used to do a lot of cookie baking with my mother. It

was my way of getting to eat the dough. My favorite ones were any that had chocolate in them. She would always scold me that raw cookie dough wasn't healthy, but I'd do it anyway when her back was turned."

They chatted together as they went back down the stairs to the kitchen. The original brick flooring of the kitchen was intact, though treated to resist stains these days, and it shone under a freshly dried coat of wax. The chef gave a last swipe with her mop in front of the stove. She was getting ready to leave for a couple of hours before returning in time to cook the evening dinner. Morgan waved to Brenda as she left, knowing that she didn't have to tell Brenda where to find everything.

Brenda gathered the ingredients while instructing Bryce where to find the mixing bowls and measuring utensils. At her direction, he retrieved several cookie sheets from the lower cabinet of the long woodblock table.

"I think we're ready to get started. I'll start with oatmeal raisin and you can do the chocolate chip ones. Just don't eat all the dough so we'll have enough." Brenda passed him a recipe card and set the oatmeal raisin recipe card in front of her, though she hardly needed to read it, she knew it so well.

"I figured you'd want to make some plain ones we could decorate."

"That's coming. I want at least three dozen sugar cookies so they can be decorated."

They got busy and for the first few minutes they worked without words. Brenda was impressed that Bryce really did know how to bake cookies. He read the recipe once and easily followed it until two cookie sheets were covered with the results.

"I know you want to ask about Jenny and me," Bryce said as they worked.

It was true Brenda was curious, but she had decided she didn't want to get involved in the bizarre turn of events in the relationship. "I'm curious of course, but you don't have to explain things to me."

"I made a fool of myself, truth be told," he said. "I don't know what I was thinking turning to Molly. Jenny is a wonderful girl and my true love. Molly is very sweet, and attractive, too, but I've come to regret my bad behavior."

"Shouldn't you be explaining this to Jenny?"

"I plan to have a good long talk with her soon. I went to her shop to find her yesterday, and got out a few awkward words, but she was very busy. Everyone is ordering their Christmas flowers from Blossoms. Her employee who usually works in the afternoons went home sick so she was alone."

"I have to admit I'm baffled as to how it all came about.

You and Jenny seemed meant for one another. What in the world happened that you decided to suddenly switch partners like that?"

Bryce slid the two cookie sheets into the oven and set the timer. He wiped his hands on a nearby dish towel and sighed before he answered her. "Pete and I have been close friends ever since I moved back here from Brooklyn. He was the first to suggest I date Molly and see how it went. At first the girls were doubtful, but later Jenny told me she found Pete attractive enough to give it a try. So before we knew it...we had switched."

Brenda didn't respond. Bryce Jones was known to be the biggest flirt in history around Sweetfern Harbor. Pete Graham was known to be a town gossip, but he was otherwise level-headed. Something inside her told her the events had happened the other way around.

"Why would you leave Jenny? More than once we've heard you declare your love for her. Was it all fake? This wasn't all your idea, was it, Bryce?"

His eyes grew wide. "It was all Pete's idea. I'm guilty for going along with it, it's true. But Jenny agreed to try it out, too."

Brenda was bothered by his explanation. She hoped to get to hear Jenny's side of the story in private soon. Perhaps the young girl had felt pressured and did not want to admit that to her father, but she might say it if

Brenda let on that she understood the situation. The timer chimed just then, and Bryce donned oven mitts to take out the sheets of delicious cookies. A mouth-watering aroma filled the kitchen.

Brenda suggested they take a platter of the cookies to the foyer area and a tray into the sitting room. Though the rooms weren't all booked, there was still a handful of guests around.

"I'll carry them out," Bryce said. "Don't forget you have one more tray in the oven." He looked at the timer. "It looks like another five minutes and they'll be done. They sure taste good," he said.

Brenda didn't miss the twinkling eyes and was even more convinced the young detective could win anyone over just by his charm and good looks. "Thanks for your help. After you put those trays out, come back to the kitchen and pour yourself another cup of coffee to go and take a few cookies with you."

"I will," Bryce said. "I'm on duty tonight at the police station. It will keep me awake." He laughed and when he came back from dropping off the trays, he told Brenda he would leave through the back door. He grabbed two chocolate chip cookies from the tray on his way out.

"He sure is good-looking," Allie said, appearing in the kitchen door. She appeared ready to physically swoon.

"If my mom would let me date older guys, he'd be my pick."

"He's already taken, Allie," Brenda said. "Besides, one day you'll find your own dream man, someone meant just for you."

She took the last tray of cookies out to cool and told Allie she was going up to her apartment until dinner time. Once inside her door, she pulled the first box over to her easy chair. Then, after preparing a cup of tea, she settled down to look through its contents. Just then, a knock on her door interrupted her.

"Come on in," she called out. Her father Tim Sheffield walked in and looked lovingly at his daughter. Brenda offered him hot tea or coffee.

"If you have coffee, I'll take a cup."

He observed the large boxes stacked near the door and the one Brenda had obviously just opened. He held something behind his back until they settled in her comfortable living area. Brenda asked what he was hiding from her.

"I have your wedding gift. Every bride has to have something old, right? I thought this would please you." Tim held a familiar gold-leafed box that once set on her mother's dresser. He opened it and pulled out a pearl necklace that gleamed softly in the winter light. "I bought this pearl necklace for your mother. I saw it in an antique shop and knew it was something she would like to have. It's from 1953. She loved pearls. I thought that you'd like to have it now, unless you didn't intend to wear a necklace on your wedding day."

Brenda held the necklace and looked up at her father with shining eyes. "I hadn't thought about jewelry yet and this solves it. I love it and will cherish it forever. It's beautiful. It will be like having her right there with me on my wedding day." She got up and gave her father a hug. "Thank you, Dad. It is so thoughtful. I love you."

Both father's and daughter's eyes misted. Brenda fingered the delicate necklace as memories flooded over her.

Tim stood up and said he was going for a refill. "What do you have in all these boxes?"

"They are decorations and other stuff William thought I might like to have here. I'm getting ready to delve in and see what treasures are inside. I still have plenty of trunks and boxes to go through in the attic that belonged to Uncle Randolph. You might like to do that with me soon."

Tim came back into the room and handed his daughter a fresh cup of hot tea. "The last time I saw Randolph was a little over five years ago, right here at Sheffield Bed and Breakfast. Staying here has made me realize how much I miss my brother. I regret the estrangement I caused between us. I seem to be good at creating division at times." He smiled regretfully at Brenda. "He was very different from me, but even I admitted how much talent he had. He was very creative not only in the theater but right here as well. He understood the significance of his investment and recognized the value this Queen Anne mansion held as a bed and breakfast."

They briefly discussed their memories of Randolph and then Brenda moved on to another subject she wondered if her father had any input on.

"Phyllis asked me to see if I could find out what happened to her long-lost brother. Patrick Lindsey disappeared without a trace five years ago. It may have been around the time you visited Uncle Randolph here. Do you have any memory of this incident with Patrick's disappearance?"

Tim thought back. "I was only here in Sweetfern Harbor a very short time. I had a run nearby and decided to drop in to see my brother for a few days before heading home. My vacation came up that July and I wanted to spend it all with you and your mother, so I didn't stick around here very long." He leaned back in his chair. "I do recall Patrick Lindsey. I met him briefly. I remember Randolph telling me Patrick had some kind of a bet going on with Pete Graham. It had to do with an apartment downtown."

Brenda sat forward. "Do you mean the apartment that Patrick lived in?"

"The thing I remember most is that when I met Patrick we chatted about general things. Mostly about the climate here, things like that. Then Pete Graham came up and was very rude."

"What do you mean?" Brenda couldn't recall the town's affable mailman ever showing signs of rudeness.

"He interrupted us and looked directly at me. He told me not to poke my nose in their business. I was stunned, to say the least. But worse yet, I never got a chance to ask anyone about it, because a day later Randolph confronted me and told me to leave and we got into a huge argument. That was the day I made the decision to never come back here. I don't know why Randolph willed the place to you, Brenda, but I see how happy you are. Your happiness helps me let go of the bad things that happened between Randolph and me."

"I'm horrified at what you are telling me," Brenda said, her mind racing. "I had no idea why you didn't like it here, but it all makes sense to me now. Did you and Randolph ever speak again?"

"When I got home, I felt badly about the way we parted. I wrote him several letters apologizing about our arguments before I left. He never answered any of my letters. I tried calling him once, but he didn't answer. It is still very strange to me, and I guess I'll never know exactly what happened. As for Patrick, I had no idea he went missing. Now I wonder if that happened at the same time all of the uproar was going on between Randolph and me." Tim shook his head. "I still have no idea why he told me to leave."

"I'm wondering about Pete Graham," Brenda said. "I've never known him to lose his temper or show bad behavior like you describe. Do you think he and Randolph had anything to do with Patrick suddenly leaving Sweetfern Harbor?"

"Your guess is as good as mine. It was all very strange at the time and now that we talk about it, it still makes no sense to me."

Brenda wondered who she could talk to that might know more about these events, but meanwhile, she had another unexplained mystery nagging at her. She explained to her father her interest in finding out what the boxes contained. "I think William knows that there is more than decorations in them. Do you want to help me solve the mystery?"

Tim agreed to help out. Brenda told him her hunch was that Lady Pendleton may have somehow been involved in Patrick's disappearance. She told him how Phyllis's brother had won in court over the wealthy and controlling woman. This only piqued Tim's interest in the case at hand. Together, they pulled out the bubble wrap that covered the contents. Several Hallmark ornaments still in unopened boxes were set aside. After several more layers of ornaments, Brenda's eyes lit up.

She held up a large, unlabeled manila envelope for her father to see.

"Is this your eureka moment?" Tim asked.

"It could be."

The large manila envelope was sealed. Brenda opened it and pulled out three letters, still with their opened envelopes. She hesitated for a moment when she read the addresses on each of them. All were addressed to Lady Pendleton. Tim and Brenda remained silent. Her hands shook as she opened the earliest dated letter. She read it aloud.

"I am reminding you of the promised money. All things are on hold until you pay up. Pete Graham."

Brenda looked at her father wonderingly. He shook his head as if he didn't know what to make of it either. She opened the second one and read: "You promised the money and you will be held to it. Do you want to do it Saturday? Pete."

Blank glances were exchanged again. "Let's see what this last one has to say," Brenda said. "Maybe it will make more sense."

She opened it and read it. "Everything has been taken care of. My father Edward will be giving the keys back to you. Pete Graham."

"Do you know what keys he is referring to?" Tim asked.

"I don't know for sure. But I do know that Patrick worked in Edward Graham's office. He was Lady Pendleton's lawyer, when she was alive. Patrick had another lawyer representing him in the case. Patrick did live in an apartment downtown. I don't know for sure, but it must have been one owned by Lady Pendleton, since he was suing her over a rent increase. I was told when I first arrived here that she owned most of the property around town, if not all of it."

"Did she own this bed and breakfast?"

"No, that was one piece of property she never got her hands on."

"There is one obvious thing," Tim said. "Lady Pendleton, Pete Graham and Edward Graham were all involved with something mysterious. They have that in common."

"There's a lot to think about, Dad. Why don't we go take a walk and breathe in some of that soothing salt air?" Brenda needed time to think things out. She folded the letters back up and put them in the envelopes. Then she put the manila envelope that held them into her bureau drawer. "Once I go through the other two boxes I may know more. But for now, I think you are right and I need time to mull it all over. I don't want to make any mistakes."

"You go ahead and take your walk, Brenda. Think things

out. I'll join your chef and see what goodies she has for me to sample."

Brenda hugged her winter coat close to her and smiled. She recalled how often in her childhood she and her father made up mysteries to be solved. It was a game between them and they could go quite deeply into the pretend crimes. This time they were looking into something very real.

CHAPTER FIVE

THE SEARCH

*B*renda had not talked to Mac recently about the mystery of the missing Patrick Lindsey. But now she felt she had enough to give him from her own detective work and it was time to give him a call.

"I have the afternoon off since I'm working tonight," Mac said. "I'll come over and you can show me what you have. I'd like to see this case resolved. Five years is much too long with no leads."

Brenda left word with Phyllis and Allie to tell the detective to come up to her apartment when he arrived. She heard his footsteps coming down the plank floorboards of the hallway and waited at the door. She opened it to the greeting of a lingering kiss. She pushed back and laughed.

"We have work to do, Detective." She pulled the envelope from the drawer and handed it to him. While he opened the first one she explained how she got them. "I think William knew about these letters. He was going through Lady Pendleton's things and said he was making room for Phyllis. He had to have seen them."

They sat in silence while Mac read each letter. "This all looks very suspicious. I think we should begin with the lawyer. I'll give him a call and tell him I want to stop by. We'll have to have a talk with Pete some time, too."

They went downstairs and out into the frigid December air, the envelope in Mac's hand. Mac opened the car door for Brenda. They chatted about possibilities on their way to Edward Graham's office. After exhausting the subject they realized neither of them had anything concrete yet to go on. At Edward's building, they went inside the plush office. Large plants fanned across the expansive window in the front lobby. The clerk buzzed Edward and then told them to go on in.

Edward was moving papers around on his desk and turned to put something inside a file drawer. He greeted Mac over his shoulder and his eyes opened wide with surprise when he turned around and saw Brenda.

"How nice to see you both. I'm in a bit of a hurry," Edward said by way of apology. "I've had reservations for a Christmas getaway since last January."

Mac was unruffled. "This won't take long."

Edward gestured for them to sit down. He sat across from them. His mahogany desk looked like something that someone much higher in status would have. Brenda was sure it was courtesy of Lady Pendleton.

"I'm interested in details of the court case Lady Pendleton had against Patrick Lindsey," Brenda said. "I understand it concerned a dispute about high rent on the apartment he rented from her. Also, I understand he won the case against her. Can you tell us anything else about it?"

Edward fingered a pen and put it back down. He picked it up again, deep in thought, and then shrugged his shoulders.

"There's not much to tell that the public records don't already show. He won the case, which meant the rent increase could not be enforced, end of story. That apartment is just upstairs from this office, actually. But then he suddenly disappeared and no one could find him. I understand that after so long a time, the case went cold. Patrick was prone to being an unsettled man. Most people decided he had taken off someplace to be alone. I don't think anyone thought much of his actions."

It bothered her that he seemed to focus more on Patrick's reputation than on how Lady Pendleton might have been involved. "I know one person who is still grief-stricken over his departure. His sister Phyllis. He left without a word to her of explanation. Phyllis still misses him as if it were yesterday," Brenda said.

"Of course," Edward said. "It is only normal she would still be upset at the way he just up and left. You would think he'd at least have told his sister goodbye. But that's the way he was, always restless."

"I recall it was Lady Pendleton's habit to raise rents on a whim," Mac said. "I admired Patrick for taking a stand on behalf of everyone who had to bow to her demands. He did what others wanted to do."

"She often raised rents, yes. I was her lawyer, as you know, but I'm glad she's gone. She was the biggest client headache I ever had. I was always shuffling papers for her. I just finished cleaning out the last of my papers that pertained to Lady Pendleton. I have to say it's a huge relief."

"I'd like to see the apartment Patrick rented," Brenda said.

"I'll have to let Pete know you are going into it first. He lives there now. My office is the only business in this building, which I purchased when it finally became available on the market after Lady Pendleton's death. The rest of the building is made up of housing units, but I can't just let anyone walk into someone's apartment."

Mac made a mental note to get a search warrant if

necessary. "Why don't you get his permission then?" Mac said. "Give me a call when you have it."

On their way back to Sheffield Bed and Breakfast, Brenda acknowledged the one thing they learned, and that was that Pete Graham now lived in Patrick's old apartment. "I wonder if Patrick's disappearance had anything to do with Pete wanting that apartment."

"I don't know the answer to that. I do know I have more to go on now than I did yesterday. I'd like to see this case come to an end. I hope Patrick is alive and well, most of all." He parked the car. "I'd like to see more of what you have in those boxes if you can spare a little time."

They went upstairs to Brenda's apartment. Phyllis offered to bring refreshments up to them. She felt the two were on to something. If anyone could find her brother, it was Brenda Sheffield. Mac and Brenda had begun digging into the second box when Phyllis knocked on the door. Brenda thanked her and set the tray on the coffee table in front of her loveseat. Phyllis didn't comment on anything but saw they were hard at work and left them with a lighter heart.

"Here are some legal-looking papers," Brenda said. She handed them to Mac.

His breath came out as a whistle. "According to this, that apartment building is worth a million dollars. Lady Pendleton was the owner."

Brenda pictured the building downtown in her mind. It had to be one of the first buildings of that size constructed in Sweetfern Harbor. The building itself appeared nondescript, brick and stonework. The architecture was the same Victorian style as the other buildings on the street.

"Is the place really worth that much?" she asked. "I have a few payments left on this place, but the original price wasn't anywhere near that amount."

"It might be worth that much today, or even more, but back then the price would have been much lower. I have a feeling Lady Pendleton forced Edward to appraise it at this higher price. She probably had him fake more appraisals like that around town." Mac glanced at his watch. "I'd better be going, Brenda. It's almost time for me to check in for my night duty at the office." He offered to help pick up the contents of the box but Brenda told him she was going to stay with it a while longer. He kissed her and left. Brenda spent a little while longer reading through the appraisal documents, but it was getting late, and she soon headed to bed.

The next morning, Brenda went downstairs and met Phyllis on the landing. Her housekeeper smiled at her. Brenda wondered how Phyllis could be so cheerful so early in the morning.

"I want to ask you a lot of questions, Brenda, but I'll hold off. It won't be easy, but I'll wait to get details from you when you have them. Just give me a hint...are you getting closer?"

"We have found a few things that may pertain to Patrick's vanishing but we're not sure anything is connected yet. I'll let you know as soon as I have anything concrete. I will tell you that Mac's interest has been given a boost. He's hopeful. But no promises."

Brenda didn't want to give her friend hope only to have it dashed again. She had to be careful. She gave Phyllis a reassuring hug.

"I'm going to have breakfast and then check in with Allie. After that, if anyone is looking for me, I'll be at the library."

Brenda knew the librarian had a wealth of knowledge about Sweetfern Harbor and its residents, past and present. She called Mrs. Perch and asked if she could spare a few moments for her. The older lady answered with enthusiasm. "Brenda, I am always available to you. Come on down, first chance you get."

After breakfast, Brenda headed straight for the library. The petite grey-haired lady pushed her glasses down on her nose and waved at Brenda when she came in. Mrs. Perch's chin rose only a little above the counter when she stood. "How can I help you, my dear?"

"I'm interested in finding out more about Patrick Lindsey. As I'm sure you know, he is the brother of my housekeeper, Phyllis Lindsey."

Brenda heard the slight sympathetic clicking of tongue from the woman. She shook her head and furrowed her brow.

"It's a mystery what happened to him. As I understand it from many, he wasn't someone to just up and leave without telling anyone. He liked to boast and if he thought something better waited for him away from here, he would have told anyone willing to listen to him." She tutted in sympathy again. "He worked here for me for a while. He was an avid reader in history especially."

"I have heard he was likeable," Brenda said. "Was he nice to work with?"

"Oh, yes, he was a nice person. He even came by here to visit with me several times after he left to work for Edward Graham. He wanted to tell me all about an apartment building he wanted to move into. It's down near Main Street, over the lawyer's office where he was working. At the time, Lady Pendleton owned that building. I would have cautioned him from renting from her, but the truth is that she owned the vast majority of rental properties here. He would have had a hard time finding a place not in her name."

"I know you also recall the lawsuit Patrick leveled against

Lady Pendleton. It seems she wanted to raise his rent as she had numerous times before."

Mrs. Perch nodded. "She often did that until anyone who rented her properties was left almost destitute. She liked her money but I think she liked harassing others more. I suppose I shouldn't speak like that of the dead, but she was a hard woman to get along with."

"Did you know that the apartment building Patrick lived in was appraised at a million dollars after Lady Pendleton bought it?"

The librarian's face registered shock at first and then she laughed. "Someone has been giving you information that's not true. There is no way that building was worth that much back then. I'm sure it's worth that much and more today, but back then, properties simply didn't command those kinds of prices. In fact, as far as I know, back then there was no property in town valued like that, unless you count the Pendleton estate. I suppose with all the acreage around it, plus the mansion, it's very possible it was worth over a million, even back then."

"I'm going to go to the city tax collector's office and see what is on file there." Brenda thanked Mrs. Perch and turned to leave.

"You can do that, but I don't think you will find any papers that assessed that building in the millions, or anywhere near it. Besides, Patrick Lindsey would have been charged a horrendous rent amount in a building assessed with that kind of value."

Brenda turned to smile at her. "I'm sure you are right about that. Thank you again."

She walked out of the library into the sunshine and the crisp air. In the distance, clouds formed and she was sure Sweetfern Harbor was in for another snowstorm by nightfall. She decided to walk to the police station so she could think things through.

Maybe Patrick suspected Lady Pendleton of falsifying the building's value and threatened to call her on it publicly in court. That was a possible motive for Lady Pendleton to want Patrick to disappear. But all of this was pure speculation. Brenda needed proof. Once inside the police station, she first saw Bryce and Chief Bob Ingram. They both greeted her.

"If you can spare a few minutes, Chief, I'd like to see the case file regarding Patrick Lindsey's disappearance."

Chief Ingram told Bryce to go ahead and find a suspect they were looking to question on a matter. Together, the chief and Brenda walked downstairs and he unlocked the metal door that led to the file storage room. Brenda stood and looked at the rows of shelves that held boxes and boxes of individual files.

"Don't worry. Everything is alphabetized, so it shouldn't be too hard to find what you're looking for. We are slowly getting it all onto the computers, but we still keep hard copies for back-up as well." He gestured down the aisle that held Patrick's case. "Also, we have some cold case files in here and you can't scan physical evidence into a computer." He laughed at his own joke and Brenda chuckled.

When they got to the end of the aisle, the chief stopped. The section where Patrick's file should have been was virtually empty. A few loose papers and items were there, but no box.

"Who has access to this area?" Brenda looked around her.

"All of us on the police force who work inside the building. Lawyers sometimes come down here, because it often helps their case in court, but they sign in and out and they can't take any files with them. Even the officers have to sign for files they take out. No files are allowed to leave the premises."

"I suppose that includes Edward Graham," Brenda stated.

"Yes, he often is down here." The chief peered again into the empty spot. "It is unusual that anything from here is kept out overnight. It would have to go directly through me in that rare case. I'll check to see who came for the file."

They went back upstairs and Chief Ingram asked his clerk for the ledger. Edward Graham had not been in the file storage room since two months earlier. He signed in to view evidence for another case, not Patrick Lindsey's. No one was noted as viewing the Lindsey file since Patrick's disappearance.

"I think it may be a good idea to dust for fingerprints in the empty spot," Brenda said, her gut telling her something more was going on here.

The chief raised his eyebrows and then agreed. She told him of the visit she and Mac had made to Edward Graham. "I hate to say it, Chief, but there was something just not right about Edward's demeanor. I've never seen him that way."

"I'll get the kit and we can go back down," he said. "I didn't realize you were taking an interest in Patrick's vanishing act."

"I don't think it was an act...but you could be right. There is more to do but some of what I've found lately sheds more light on it."

She watched as the chief dusted for prints. Then Brenda took a second look. There was Lady Pendleton's appointment book in the back of the shelf, almost invisible in the gloom. Perhaps whoever took the files mistakenly left it behind, along with the few other scattered papers on the shelf that held nothing of interest. Brenda recognized the appointment book because when Lady Pendleton died in front of the bed and breakfast, slumped over the steering wheel of her car, it was Brenda who first saw that she was dead. This appointment book was on the passenger seat of the car and Brenda recalled seeing it placed into an evidence bag. The book was not in any bag now.

"If you put this into an evidence bag for me, do you mind if I take it with me to Mac's office and thumb through it? I'll wear gloves. I know we looked at it when she died, but it may be important to look for any appointments that had to do with Patrick Lindsey. Whoever took Patrick's file was clearly interested in her appointment book, but left it behind accidentally."

Chief Bob Ingram trusted Brenda implicitly. She had worked on more than one case with his department and he knew her expertise. He did as she suggested, but not before both of them searched the shelves again to make sure nothing else was amiss.

"Edward Graham is planning to leave soon for his Christmas vacation. I feel strongly that he is somehow involved in Patrick's disappearance." She waited for the chief to respond, but he seemed to be thinking hard about it. It was no small thing to suspect the town's well-respected lawyer of something like this. "He may be someone to keep an eye on until we can go through this appointment book with a fine-toothed comb again. I think there is something in the book that will lead us forward." They climbed the stairs back to the main floor.

"I agree with you after all you've told me so far. Mac isn't in the office today. He went down to New York to look into a case. You can use his office to go through it and take as long as you need. We can even make photocopies if you want to."

"That would be helpful," Brenda said. She stood back while the chief unlocked Mac's office door. Bryce greeted them and told the chief he had a report to give him on their latest suspect in a case of theft, so they left her to her work.

Brenda sat at Mac's desk and donned a pair of gloves from the box she knew Mac kept in a drawer, then opened the appointment book. Everything looked normal. She hardly expected her to list "Blackmail at 3pm" alongside salon appointments and other usual things. She flipped to the back of the book and realized it also contained a ledger of rent collected. She kept thumbing through and leaned forward to read the tiny, neat handwriting. She realized there was only one renter listed, and that was Patrick Lindsey.

Bryce appeared at the door. "If you want help, I can help you with whatever you are looking for."

"I could use someone to play devil's advocate with me."

"I'm good at that." The young detective sat across from Brenda and waited.

"There is something suspicious about the fact that Lady

Pendleton only listed one renter in the back of her appointment book. It was Patrick Lindsey."

"That's not so unusual. She probably had another, more detailed ledger at home to keep everything in."

Brenda's look told him it was a lame explanation. He snapped on a pair of gloves himself, took the book and looked for himself. At that moment, a business card fell from the pages. It was Patrick's card. He had his own business card from the time he worked for the lawyer, evidently.

Everything was about Patrick in the back of this book, thought Brenda. No one else is listed despite her many, many rental properties around town. What made Patrick's rent different?

Brenda and Bryce were silent as they looked at the business card with Patrick's name on it. Brenda handed it to the detective.

"Why did Patrick have business cards made up?" Bryce asked.

"He worked for Edward Graham. I suppose it was Edward's idea to give his position a sort of prestige. According to Phyllis, her brother liked the work in the lawyer's office." Still, it wasn't enough. Brenda hoped that the longer they kept going, the more they would find.

CHAPTER SIX

SUSPECTS

*B*renda flipped the pages back to Lady Pendleton's appointments immediately before her death. There were blank pages every three or four pages for her notes. Lady Pendleton was meticulous in noting personal information concerning Patrick. His full address was listed, along with a phone number. When she looked closer, she realized that there were also details of delivery dates and times listed over a span of many weeks. Brenda guessed that Patrick often took legal materials to the courthouse or to the police department on behalf of Edward. Lady Pendleton had listed each day and the time of day he left the office for this purpose and when he returned.

"My initial conclusion after reading this is that Lady

Pendleton kept track of Patrick's every move because of his lawsuit against her," Bryce said.

"I have another hunch," Brenda said. "Just after Patrick left, I think there's a reason it was Pete Graham who moved right into that same apartment. Maybe Lady Pendleton paid him off to gossip against Patrick around town. He probably lived there rent-free in exchange for that job. We all know what a gossip Pete Graham is. He takes advantage of his mail route to spread word about everyone around town."

"And people listen to him, too," Bryce said.

Brenda leaned back in Mac's comfortable desk chair. "I sometimes doubt that Edward Graham resented Lady Pendleton as much as he claims, though he clearly wanted Mac and me to believe that. What if Pete was easy to acquire because Edward is his father and Edward was her lawyer?"

"So you're saying Lady Pendleton and Edward Graham were partners in the rent raises?"

Brenda nodded. "They were conspiring together, as in partners." Brenda told Bryce about the value set on the apartment building Pete lived in. Bryce's eyes popped open.

"That place was valued at a million dollars back then?" Again, Brenda nodded.

Both of them looked up quickly when the door opened.

"You two look comfortable in here," Mac said. He came around his desk and kissed Brenda. She explained that the chief told her to use his office. "I already heard that," Mac said. Brenda started to get up and give him his chair. "Sit back down and bring me up to date on everything."

Brenda told Mac everything she had discovered so far. "We have a motive that places Edward, Pete and Lady Pendleton in the middle of Patrick's disappearance."

"Edward told us he's leaving town. Do you recall if he said when?" Mac asked.

"I don't know for sure, but I believe tonight or tomorrow. He was in a hurry to get rid of us, don't you think? He kept saying he had to pack up."

Without another word, Mac rushed from his office and approached the chief. After a quick consultation, Bob Ingram called over several more officers. He directed them to look for Pete Graham and bring him in for questioning. Next, the chief told Bryce to go with Mac and bring Edward Graham to the police station.

"If he's not at home or in his office, then go to the airport. He'll have to get the shuttle to New York if he's going to fly commercial to the Islands. I'll get the airport alerted as well as the bus and train stations, just in case."

The three men looked at Brenda expectantly. She told

them she would wait until the men were brought in for questioning. She wanted to spend more time alone going through the appointment book. Brenda believed in getting every detail ready to present to the chief and his detectives before any interrogations. They hurried out and she returned to Mac's office.

Brenda went to the front of the book and read each page slowly and carefully. Lady Pendleton's handwriting was distinct and easy to read where she made notes in the ensuing pages. She had listed the times Patrick left and returned to the lawyer's office, down to the minute. Brenda felt sure Lady Pendleton wasn't following him herself. Someone reported to her and that someone was most likely either Pete or his father, or both.

She recalled Edward's remark regarding the case that Patrick won against the most powerful woman in town. He said the missing persons case had gone cold after Patrick had vanished without word. But why didn't Lady Pendleton sue for missing rent payments? That could only go unnoticed if someone knew Patrick was no longer alive. She rested her head in her hands and hoped Phyllis's brother wasn't dead. Above all, she wanted to bring him to her friend's wedding alive and well. What if she dug further into this case only to find out that he had been dead all this time?

The police station was quiet for the most part. Brenda heard a cop bring someone in who apparently had too much to drink. She heard the officer tell him to sleep it off as he closed the cell door and that they would talk later. The more she read the appointment notes, the more her curiosity grew. There was nothing new to discover, but going over it again planted new energy into her speculations. Mac's voice reached her.

"You'll go in this room, Edward," he was saying out in the corridor.

Brenda left the office and joined the group of officers. Edward and Pete were separated into two different interrogation rooms. She opted to stand behind the one-way glass and listen. No amount of persuasion made Edward admit to having anything to do with Patrick Lindsey's disappearance. Mac told him they had evidence he was involved. Edward simply shook his head and stated there was no evidence that existed. He played it cool the entire session. She knew that he likely knew the process so well that he would call for his own lawyer if they dared ask him one question too many. He was probably just biding his time. Brenda moved to the window in front of the interrogation room where Pete Graham sat. He answered questions in the same manner as his father had. It struck Brenda as odd. Pete was certainly not a practiced lawyer, but he was cool as a cucumber. It was as if they had practiced this scenario more than once.

She finally left the police station. She had to get more

information than she had found so far and knew who to talk to. Molly Lindsey and Pete Graham had been an item for months. Everyone in Sweetfern Harbor expected them to marry any day. After that long of a courtship, even with the recent strange switch of partners, surely Pete would have told Molly something pertinent about her uncle. Maybe Molly heard something that involved Patrick's disappearance but simply hadn't put it together yet. Brenda walked to Morning Sun Coffee. Molly greeted her and brought a cup of coffee to her. The shop was sparsely occupied and when Brenda asked Molly if she had time for a chat, she agreed.

"I have some questions about Pete. What kind of a man is he really?"

Molly laughed at the question. "He is what most people see. He's very nice and courteous to everyone. He loves the mail route and how everyone expects him to bring news along with their mail." She chuckled. "His one flaw is possibly that he is quite the gossip around town. But I don't mind that. He knows things before anything gets printed in the newspaper."

"Does he ever show a...quirky side? I mean, does he ever appear to be hiding something?" Brenda explained her question. "Certainly he has a flaw besides gossiping. Everyone has more than one."

"He is as I told you. He has a few health problems, but nothing serious. His knee gives him trouble sometimes but that's probably because he's been walking that mail route for the last several years. I've heard many postal workers who have routes have knee or hip problems. He has asthma, too. I know he has prescriptions for pain and for his asthma."

"I'm like a lot of people around here," Brenda said, "wondering why you and Pete were waiting to get married. And then I saw you and Bryce are interested in one another lately. It's all a mystery to me."

Molly cast her eyes down momentarily, fiddling with her fingernails. "Just after my mother became engaged to William, I brought up the subject of marriage with Pete. I was ready to move in with him. At first he seemed okay with it all and then a couple of days later he told me that Bryce came to him with an unusual idea. That had to do with us switching couples. He thought we should at least try it. I liked Bryce, and Jenny seemed to like Pete, so the four of us decided to give it a try." She glanced at Brenda and her carefree tone faded a little. "I didn't like the idea at first. I loved Pete, but I got the distinct impression he was nowhere near ready for marriage. I thought it might be a good thing to date someone else, at least temporarily. I made sure Jenny was agreeable to it all."

To Brenda this was the craziest explanation yet. She reminded herself that even if she wouldn't have gone for it, the four involved must have each had their own reasons.

"So you are telling me that Bryce suggested the idea, not Pete."

"That's what Pete told me. It was set up to be a trial period. I think Jenny wasn't all that happy with the idea at first, like me, but she agreed. She and I thought it was meant to be a diversion...you know, to allow all of us to get to know one another better. Jenny is a very good friend of mine. I went along with it once she agreed."

"Did Pete and your uncle get along well?"

"As far as I know they did. Uncle Patrick came in here regularly and often Pete joined him at the table on his break. The only odd thing that ever crossed my mind was that right after my uncle left town with no word, Pete decided to move into that apartment. I don't think my mother ever went there after he disappeared. She was told he had taken all of his belongings with him so there was no reason. Besides, it upset her a lot."

"Did you ever go to the apartment after Pete moved there?"

Molly held up her hand. "I only went once. That was enough for me. Pete Graham is no housekeeper. He had lived there about a week when I went there. It looked like a war zone. There were a few dishes in the sink that hadn't been washed even though he had a dishwasher. I guess it can be described as a typical bachelor pad." She smiled and shook her head.

Brenda didn't see humor in the story. Either Pete Graham had nothing to hide or he was a very good actor. He may put on a good show for everyone to build his nice guy reputation but there was something suspicious about him that Brenda couldn't put her finger on. She took the last sip of her coffee and declined a refill, thanking Molly for her frankness.

Once outside, she called Mac. The interrogations were finished. He told her that they weren't allowing Edward or Pete Graham to leave town. "Edward wasn't happy about it, but agreed to hold off for another few days. We were surprised he agreed. He knows he's not under arrest. It's like playing cat and mouse when you have a lawyer as a possible suspect. But at least this gives us time to get into it all deeper."

"I do wonder if Lady Pendleton ever mentioned anything to William about Patrick's disappearance."

"I've got time to go see him right now," Mac said. "I'll see what he has to say. But we all know they didn't exactly have a close relationship."

"I agree. But maybe he has found more papers that pertain to it all. You can tell him what my father and I found in the box he sent home with me, and what you and I found, too. I feel sure he knew what was in there." She paused. "By the way, there was a key in the packet I found. I have it with me but I'm not sure what it goes to."

"Maybe it's an apartment key," Mac said. "Keep it with you so we'll know where it is. I may get a search warrant to go inside Patrick's former apartment. During the interrogation of Pete, I didn't think to tell him I wanted to look inside," he said with a grin. "Besides, I didn't want to tip him off, though his father has probably already done that."

Brenda passed the apartment building on her way back to the Sheffield Bed and Breakfast and couldn't resist going for a closer look. Patrick's address, found in Lady Pendleton's appointment book, indicated he lived on the top floor, now occupied by Pete Graham. She felt luck was with her because the apartment was on the backside of the building. She realized that Patrick must have had a wonderful view of the ocean from this vantage point. She wondered if Pete Graham appreciated it, too. Brenda noticed that Edward's office was closed. The lights were out and she presumed he had gone home after the interrogation. She knew Pete would be at the post office finishing up work. She had a few hours before he would be home.

The front door at the opposite end of the building was unlocked. She went inside and climbed the stairs to the top floor. Pulling the key from her purse she inserted it into the lock. After several attempts, she faced the reality that it didn't fit. She looked down the hall. Every door resembled the one she stood at. The only sounds came from the seagulls and the ocean lapping against the town's harbor wall down the street.

Giving up on finding any significant information, Brenda started to go back downstairs when she noticed a trash can in the corner of the landing. Trash almost filled the container. Her eye caught something that caused her hopes to rise. The pill bottle was partially hidden beneath torn paper and when she retrieved it she saw Edward Graham's name on the prescription label. The empty bottle had contained Restoril. She knew this pill was one that not only helped people fall asleep but also helped them stay asleep. She was familiar with it since her mother had used that prescription on occasion. Why would Edward Graham need sleeping pills? Brenda reminded herself not to judge too quickly when thoughts raced through her mind. She knew it wasn't necessarily a sign of a guilty conscience that someone had trouble sleeping. After all, her mother had a clear conscience, as far as Brenda knew.

She tucked the bottle into her purse and vowed to ask Edward Graham about it at the next opportunity. As quiet as the hallway was, Brenda felt sure no one was in the other four apartments on that floor. On another hunch, she went back and inserted the key into the one next to Pete's. It didn't work, nor did it work in any of the doors. Disappointed, she finally went back to the ground level and out the front door. Snow began to fall and the fresh cover over old snowfall soon looked like a new carpet.

Brenda loved winter. The cold snowflakes that hit her face rejuvenated her. She walked the rest of the block and circled back down the alley until she reached the back of the apartment building. She stood back and gazed at the structure. When she looked down she saw fresh tracks in the snow that definitely weren't her own. They didn't lead directly to the door. Instead, they ended at a section of the building's wall before turning away again. She was dumbfounded.

CHAPTER SEVEN

DISCOVERY

*B*renda stood where she was. The footprints that led to the blank brick wall and then left were fresh. Someone had made those prints while she was up on the top floor. She was baffled as to why someone would go to the wall and then turn away from it. There were no meters there or air units of any kind. She peered closer at the brick wall of the Victorian building. When she looked again, things began to fall in place. There was a tiny, dark keyhole in the wall. She fumbled in her purse and in her nervousness almost spilled its contents when she pulled the key out. She stepped in the same prints that were already there and inserted the key into the keyhole. To her surprise and dread, the key fit. What would she find? She heard the lock click and gave the wall a push.

It took several tries before Brenda successfully pushed open the hidden door. No one would have guessed it was a door camouflaged in the brick wall. Without the footprints giving the first clue to the keyhole, Brenda would have easily missed it. Lady Pendleton's former building had a special private entrance, but to what? Brenda quickly looked around her. No one was in sight. Snow was already covering the retreating footprints. She went inside and closed the door behind her.

Brenda blinked several times to adjust to the semi-darkness of the passageway. She moved forward and the floor sloped down gradually. There were several dim nightlights along the lower part of the hallway. She looked left and right and there was nothing on either side of her. The width of the hallway was approximately five feet. After walking further, she saw a wooden door a few yards ahead of her. She held her breath and listened. No one had opened the door behind her and she hoped whoever had just been in here wasn't coming back any time soon. The huge wooden door appeared thick.

Something dawned on her that sent shock waves through her body. "Patrick," she called through the keyhole in the large door. "Patrick," she called louder. She put her ear to the opening meant for an old-fashioned skeleton key. She heard a moaning sound. No one actually answered but she knew what she heard.

"Patrick, be patient a little while longer. I'll be back with help." Brenda rushed to the outside door and cautiously opened it. She ran to the end of the block and called Mac.

"I think I've found Patrick," she said. "Hurry to the back of the apartment building. Come right away. I'll meet you by the back door." She hung up before Mac could answer her. She paced in the thickening snowfall while she waited. It seemed like hours, but in reality it was mere minutes before Mac, Bryce and Chief Ingram pulled up in two patrol cars in the alley.

She motioned them over to the wall. Mac wondered what she found so interesting about the back of the brick building until he spotted the keyhole as she pointed to it.

"The key I found fits in there." Brenda inserted the small key and told them to push on the wall. Bryce nudged the hidden door open with no trouble. "Follow me." She hurried down the sloping passageway to the wooden door. Again she bent to the keyhole and called Patrick's name. A voice moaned louder. Brenda turned to the men. "Someone will have to open this door. He doesn't sound good. I don't suppose any of you has a skeleton key on you."

Without words, all three men formed a phalanx and rammed their bodies against the door. It opened on their second try. Inside the small, pitch-black room they could barely see a cot. There were no windows. To the right was a small bathroom barely large enough for one person to squeeze into. Remnants of fast food cartons were strewn on the dilapidated table near the cot. Brenda switched a lamp on that was near the bed and the dim light flooded the room. An emaciated man on the cot cowered from the light. He could barely lift his head.

"Are you Patrick Lindsey?" Brenda asked.

The figure on the cot gave a lopsided grin before closing his eyes again.

"That's Patrick," Mac said. Chief Ingram agreed.

Brenda showed them the empty sleeping pill bottle with Edward Graham's name on it. "I found this in the trash upstairs. I think he has been drugged with sleeping pills," she said. She knelt down next to the cot and placed a hand gently on his skinny arm. "It's going to be okay, Patrick," she said, and he made only a faint moan in reply.

Detective Bryce Jones left the building and called for an ambulance. In a few short minutes, the EMTs arrived and loaded Patrick Lindsey into the ambulance. The sirens blared as it headed for the hospital with its precious cargo. Two more cops had arrived and were stringing yellow tape across the doorway where Patrick Lindsey had spent the last five years. They did the same on the outside door.

"Go arrest Edward and Pete Graham right away. Charge them with kidnapping, for starters."

Chief Bob Ingram pushed his phone back into his pocket and told Brenda to get in his car. Brenda's heart was racing as they followed the ambulance. Bryce followed in his car. One of the cops rode with him and when they arrived at the hospital, he was ordered to stay with Patrick Lindsey at all times and guard his room, once he was moved to one. Chief Ingram instructed his officer to not allow anyone to enter the room unless authorized to do so.

At the hospital, Patrick was taken to Intensive Care first. "We're keeping him there until we can evaluate him better, determine whether he is seriously afflicted in some way. It's precautionary," the doctor told Chief Ingram. They were worried about his emaciated state. Brenda shuddered to think what the poor man had been through mentally, under lock and key and without any access to sunshine for five long years.

They all went to an assigned private waiting room for further news of Patrick's condition.

"I have to call Phyllis," Brenda said, realizing suddenly she had almost forgotten the ultimate purpose of her investigation. "She will be thrilled we found Patrick." She noticed a hesitation from the two men at first. "She has to know. What if he doesn't make it for some reason? She has to see him first. She's his next of kin."

"You're right, Brenda," the chief said. "Go ahead and give her the good news."

Phyllis's voice shook when she heard Brenda's news. She asked Brenda several times if she was sure it was her brother. Brenda assured her he had not only been identified by the chief and Mac but now by his own cognizance, as the hospital had been able to reverse the effects of the sedative he had been drugged with. She told the housekeeper that Patrick was in Intensive Care for observation but she could have a short visit with him. To Brenda, it seemed in no time at all Phyllis and Molly were running down the hallway of the hospital. The doctor allowed them to go in and see Patrick for a few minutes. Mixed emotions crossed Phyllis's face. She tried to hold tears back through a wide smile that spoke her joy.

Brenda paced in the small waiting room.

"You'll have to wait like the rest of us, Brenda. Pacing won't hurry things along." Mac grinned at her. "How did you find that door? I've been down that alley many times in the past and never once did I see it as anything except a part of the building."

Brenda was happy for the diversion. She explained the footprints in the snow. "They were probably two or three sizes larger than mine. Whoever made the prints has wide feet, too. I was curious why they led to the wall and then walked away back to the alley. I wondered why the person hadn't gone into the building through the main door. When I looked closer where the footsteps had

86

stopped, I saw the small black keyhole. I tried the key I found in the packet that Lady Pendleton owned and it fit. The rest is history."

She decided now was not the time to tell them she had tried the key in Pete's apartment and the others on that hallway. When asked, she explained she had learned from Lady Pendleton's appointment book that the apartment was on the backside of the Victorian building on the top floor.

"I decided to go around to the back and see if I could find any clues. I had already gone inside the building through the unlocked front door. I went up to the top floor hoping to find some clues. That's when I saw the pill bottle in the trash can."

"I don't suppose you tried that key in Pete's apartment," Mac said teasingly.

Warmth crept into Brenda's face. "I admit I tried it, but it didn't work. All right...I confess I tried the other doors on that hall as well."

The detective and Chief of Police glanced at one another with amusement but neither commented.

"We'd better see if we can talk to Patrick now," Chief Ingram said.

They met Phyllis and Molly coming from Intensive Care. Phyllis enveloped Brenda in a big hug. "He wouldn't give us any details because he said he had to talk to Mac and Bob first. He said a woman found him. I'm sure that was you, Brenda."

"I did find him. I'll give you details later. Right now, we're going to try to talk to him."

"He has IVs for fluid going into him, but he's awake," Molly said. "We're going to wait here until we can see him again."

Phyllis and Molly hugged Brenda one more time. "Thank you, Brenda," Phyllis said, her eyes tearing up. She repeated it three more times before Brenda managed to pull away and follow the two men.

In his hospital bed, Patrick was leaning against the pillows stacked behind his head and shoulders. A light tint of pinkness had returned to his face but he was still groggy. The doctor told them they had ten to fifteen minutes with him but could come back in about an hour or two.

"He should be even more alert by then. We'll be doing tests on him in a matter of a few hours."

Patrick looked at Brenda. "I only know you are the person who found me, but I don't think we've been formally introduced."

She introduced herself to Patrick and briefly explained her ownership of Sheffield Bed and Breakfast. Chief

Ingram told Patrick they were allowed just a few minutes with him but they needed some information as to how he ended up in the hole they found him in.

"I was working for Edward Graham. Lady Pendleton wanted an exorbitant rent increase from me and I took her to court over it. Edward pointed me to a lawyer outside the office to take my case. I won the case." He coughed and looked exhausted, but then resumed. "A few days later I discovered a second set of records of dealings between Edward and Lady Pendleton. It was by accident I found them."

He took a deep breath and his eyelids fluttered for a few seconds. Mac told him they could come back in about an hour. "No," Patrick said. "I want to give you a few details at least. Lady Pendleton was tampering with everyone's tax records. She looked at how much money businesses and individuals earned and then raised rents to match. There was no way anyone could get ahead, no matter how good their businesses did or their jobs increased their paychecks. She raised rents accordingly."

"I think that's enough for now. Try to sleep some," the chief said.

"No. That's all I've done the last five years," Patrick said. "I have to tell you a little more right now so you can arrest Edward and Pete, too." The chief told him they were already in custody and Patrick seemed to relax a little. He continued. "I had no idea Edward already knew when I told him what I discovered. I even asked him to instigate a lawsuit against her. I guess Edward passed this on to her and she interfered right away. Edward told me she threatened to blackmail him and eventually get him disbarred if he let me go public with everything. She told him to involve Pete in the cover-up, though Edward didn't want to do it at first." He grinned. "I guess Lady Pendleton will finally get what's really coming to her." No one gave him the news of her demise.

Patrick shifted in his bed. "Unbeknownst to me, she told Edward to get rid of me. He told Pete to intercept all mail coming to me and going out from me. Lady Pendleton knew I was looking for an apartment and she was the one who owned the building. She told Edward to show me the apartment on the top floor. I took it knowing that no matter where I lived she probably owned the building. I expected her to raise my rent like everyone else, but I knew I could go public with the evidence of her dirty tax dealings if I needed to. It was a hot July night as I recall when Pete came to see me. We had a couple of beers together. I can usually handle two with no problem, but I got drowsy and before I knew what had happened I woke up and found myself locked in that dungeon where you found me."

"I know you have a lot more to say, Patrick, but if we don't follow your doctor's orders we'll be banned from the ICU. Get a good night's sleep and we'll talk in the morning." The chief patted him on his arm. "Gain some weight back. You look too skinny."

Patrick grinned again, weakly. "Thanks for the compliment as usual, Bob." He looked at Brenda and beckoned her closer to the bed. He squeezed her hand and grew serious. "I will never be able to repay you for what you did for me."

"Yes, you will. You will be the best wedding present for your sister. You'll be able to celebrate her wedding Christmas Eve."

They left Patrick with a shocked but happy look on his face.

"Do either of you need a ride home?" Mac asked Phyllis and Molly.

"We're staying right here until we can have another visit with him," Phyllis said. "I want to make sure he doesn't disappear again."

"I told him he was your wedding wish," Brenda said. "He'll be waiting to hear details from you." She hugged Phyllis and walked down the hall with Mac and the chief. They invited her to go back to the police station with them.

"I want you in the interrogation rooms this time, Brenda," Mac said. "I think we'll start with Pete, and let Edward stew a little while."

CHAPTER EIGHT

INTERROGATIONS

*B*renda was more than ready to hear what Pete Graham had to say. She was told neither man knew that Patrick Lindsey had been rescued. This will prove interesting, she thought.

Pete sat across from Mac and Brenda. He couldn't meet their eyes. "I understand new evidence has come in on Patrick Lindsey," Mac said. "I'm thinking you are the one who killed him."

Pete's head jerked up. "He can't be dead."

"How do you know?"

It dawned on Pete he had been tricked. He drew several deep breaths but didn't speak. Brenda and Mac waited patiently.

"I have all night," Mac said. He looked at Brenda. "How about you, Brenda, do you have any place you should be right now?"

"I'm good," Brenda said. "We don't have a full house at the bed and breakfast since things are winding down for the big holiday." They continued the small talk between them about their unlimited time while Pete fidgeted.

Pete finally banged his fist on the table. "I know where Patrick has been these past five years," he said. "I can take you there and you will see that he is just fine."

"Do you describe someone as 'just fine' when they've been drugged with your father's sleeping pills? At least, with a prescription with his name on it," Brenda said. "Why would Edward Graham need sleeping pills? Did you drug Patrick Lindsey?"

Pete struggled, his face contorted with confusion, regret, and helplessness. "I...I didn't have a choice. He told me to get it done."

"To get what done?" Mac asked.

"Lady Pendleton wanted Patrick dead. He told me I had to do it." Once he had said the words, all the energy seemed to go out of Pete's body. His cheerful persona was gone and in its place Brenda saw only a sad man facing the consequences of his own cowardice. "But I couldn't kill him. So I told my dad Patrick died of an overdose and said I got rid of the body. He believed me. He was happy, since that's what Lady Pendleton wanted to happen. I knew about that storage space that was never used. I found a key for the hidden door in with the folder of illegal tax manipulation information of hers and took it, thinking I could use it for something. Later I discovered the door around back. I think she ordered it built but never knew where it was, and forgot about it." He stopped, his shoulders slumped. He finally looked up at Mac with defeat in his eyes. "I couldn't kill anyone."

Mac and Brenda remained silent. Pete continued to tell them that he paid a visit to Patrick in the middle of everything. He had the sleeping pills with him and drugged Patrick's beer. He then dragged him downstairs and around to the hidden door. He had already made sure there was a cot in there and saw that he had food and water to drink. Every time he went to Patrick's room, he found it easy to drop sleeping pills into his drinks. He usually went late at night when no one was around, or awake on that floor. Right after moving him to the hidden room, Pete had moved all of Patrick's furniture and personal items out in the middle of the night, to make it look as if he had left suddenly. He had dumped it all at a landfill several counties away.

As time went on, Pete had told his father to keep refilling the sleeping pills because he needed them to block out the bad dreams about what he had done at Lady Pendleton's behest. His father had not known the pills were for Patrick all along.

"Why did you visit him this afternoon?" Brenda locked eyes with him. "I saw footprints in the snow so I know you were there today."

Pete leaned back quickly. "Did you find him? How did you get in?"

"Never mind," Mac said. "We're the ones here to ask the questions. Why were you there today?"

"I had been lying to my father for so long. He believed Patrick was dead all these years. He never asked me where I put the body or how I managed it. I intercepted mail coming and going from Patrick for so long, too. The longer he was hidden, the more it was only incoming mail that had to be intercepted."

"When did you begin tampering with his mail?" Brenda asked.

"Lady Pendleton told my father she wanted me to start doing that from the day Patrick started working in my father's office. That was when he started the lawsuit against her. I did that with others' mail, too, so no one would suspect anything."

Brenda realized something. "Does that mean you destroyed important mail? Like maybe letters between my father and his own brother?" Pete nodded. "Do you realize the rift you caused between them? They had been close as brothers and your interference helped destroy that."

Pete admitted that was true but offered no apology. "I did what I was forced to do."

"What did you get in return for your deeds?" Mac asked.

"Lady Pendleton gave me Patrick's apartment rent-free. I was offered protection by Lady Pendleton and she paid me for doing what she asked."

"Well, that protection promise won't have any bearing now, will it?" Mac asked. "And I doubt you'll have a job at the post office. Mail tampering is a federal offense."

The interrogation room door opened and an officer handed Mac a note. He read it and passed it to Brenda. She wasn't surprised to read that Edward Graham's fingerprints were a match for the ones found on the empty shelf where Patrick Lindsey's file had been in storage.

Mac signaled for an officer to handcuff Pete Graham again and return him to his cell.

"I have another question before he goes," Brenda said. When Mac nodded, she asked Pete if he knew why Randolph threw her father out of the bed and breakfast, since he had been there that day, by all accounts. Pete told her he had lied about Tim and told Randolph his brother was sending letters back and forth to various people in Sweetfern Harbor, intending to harm his reputation and damage his bed and breakfast business.

"And how was that supposed to happen?" Brenda asked.

"I told Randolph that Tim wanted the Sheffield Bed and Breakfast and was trying to get it through a lawsuit. Of course, none of it was true, but I felt I could use him in some way in the future. Phyllis Lindsey worked for Randolph and so Randolph was naturally very interested in Patrick. I needed leverage between Tim and Randolph. That part wasn't my father's idea, or Lady Pendleton's. That was my own idea." He looked sickened by his own words.

Once outside the interrogation room, Brenda and Mac took a short break. "Let's go see Edward now," Mac said. The lawyer had time to stew, as Mac put it, but he also had time to formulate his own statement.

Mac read him his rights again. He declined a lawyer to represent him. Brenda guessed that later he would regret that decision. He seemed calm and confident.

"It looks like you are charged with kidnapping. I am adding murder and destruction of evidence to those charges," Mac said.

Edward stood suddenly, staggering back. The other officer in the room steadied his shoulders and pushed him back down into his chair. Moisture appeared on the lawyer's forehead. He rubbed both hands on his slacks.

"I don't know about any murder or these other charges you are throwing at me."

"Someone murdered Patrick Lindsey. He worked in your office just before he disappeared. You knew Lady Pendleton was illegally tampering with everyone's tax documents. I'm thinking Patrick knew what was going on and threatened to do something about it. Lady Pendleton had you under her thumb. If you didn't do everything she told you to do, your job was in jeopardy. She was unhappy about losing that lawsuit to Patrick and you were ordered to take care of him before he did any more damage to her."

Mac's eyes drilled into the man across from him.

Edward Graham's eyes flashed defiantly. "I know he is dead, but I didn't kill Patrick Lindsey. As for destroying evidence, I have no idea what you are talking about."

Mac explained that Edward's fingerprints were found in the place where Patrick Lindsey's file once was. "The file has vanished. Evidence points to the fact that you took or destroyed them. If you didn't, then we will subpoena them from you. That should take less than twenty-four hours to take care of the matter. It can be sooner, if you just tell us where they are. We already know you took them. Where are they?"

"I'll answer that only if you give me immunity. I can tell you who killed Patrick." He held up his chin in a posture of righteousness, as if he believed he held the final trump card.

Mac leaned back and clasped his hands behind his head. He turned to Brenda. "Have you ever known of a father who would sell out his own son?"

"In all the cases I've worked on back in Michigan and the ones here, I have to say I've never known a good father to do that."

Mac sat up straight again. "There is no immunity deal," he told Edward. "You didn't have to sell out your son. We know Pete told you he killed Patrick, but Patrick Lindsey is alive and well. He was rescued by Brenda and is recuperating in the hospital."

Edward's face dropped in the manner of a rock hitting the bottom of a river. His face was pale, and he had no more words for them. Mac told the other officer to take the lawyer back to his cell. "I'll be filing more charges by tomorrow," he told Edward.

Mac and Brenda remained for a few minutes where they were.

"Brenda, I love you dearly, but for the life of me I don't know how you get to the bottom of things like you do. I'm sure Bob Ingram will ask you once again to join the police force."

Brenda smiled. "I guess I just have a knack for figuring things out. But, as I've so often said, I'm happy running a bed and breakfast. More than anything, I'm happily looking forward to spending the rest of my life with you."

Mac pulled her to him and kissed her. They heard a tapping on the window and the chief came around to the door. He laughed at their realization that the window was a one-way mirror.

"You two need to go out and have some fun, this is no place for a date!" He joked. "Besides, you've spent enough time on this case today."

Both looked chagrined and brushed past the chief, who laughed at them again.

Once outside, Brenda took a deep breath. She leaned closer to Mac and gazed at the pristine wintery landscape. "I love how the snow looks when it falls so heavily. We should have quite a wonderland by morning."

"Let's go eat some Italian food and have a good glass of wine," Mac said. "I know how much you like to walk in the snow. I'll leave the car here since the restaurant is only a block away."

They nestled closer as they walked along. Brenda lifted her head and caught snowflakes on her tongue.

The aroma of pasta and simmering rich tomato sauce met their senses. They settled at a table near the window. "Tonight, we don't talk business," Mac said.

Brenda readily agreed, gazing into his eyes. As they raised a glass of wine in a toast to the beautiful snow outside, Brenda sighed happily. She knew the dinner would prove to be the relaxation both of them needed.

The next morning, Brenda went to the hospital to talk to Patrick. He had been moved from Intensive Care to a private room in another unit. An officer who knew Brenda stepped back to allow her to enter.

"You look like a new man, Patrick," she said, pleased to see him sitting up taller and looking more alert.

"I am a new man, thanks to you. I'm fully alert and ready to hear how in the world you found me. It was the luckiest day of my life."

Brenda told him of finding the envelope that belonged to Lady Pendleton and the key inside. "I tried every door on that floor and was frustrated that it didn't fit any of them. When I got back outside something drew me to the back of the building. I saw footprints in the snow that seemed to lead to the solid brick wall. I was curious and discovered the key hole. Of course, the key fit and so that's how I found you."

"I was in a stupor, I thought you were an angel at first. Those must have been Pete's footprints. He was the only person I saw for five years."

Brenda wondered how he had survived over the years, but saved those questions for later. There would be plenty of time to get to know Patrick Lindsey better. They both looked up when Phyllis and Molly came into the room. Brenda had never seen the light shining from Phyllis's face as it did that day.

"Brenda, thanks to you I have my wedding wish." Phyllis gave Brenda a quick hug and then her brother a longer one. Molly stood back and smiled at the scene, but Brenda noted sadness in her eyes.

Molly felt Brenda's eyes on her. "I still can't believe Pete would do such a thing. He lied to me all these years. He hid uncle Patrick away in that filthy little hole in the wall, away from everyone who loved him. I don't even know who Pete Graham is." She shook her head.

Phyllis turned to her daughter. "Right now, Pete Graham is a prisoner and is where he belongs. Someday you will fall in love with a man who truly deserves you. You will find love again."

Patrick told her to come to him. He gave his niece a hug. "I was duped by him, too, Molly. We will both recover. We have to. There will be two big weddings to celebrate in a very short time. We'd both better be in our best form or we may get thrown out," he joked.

"Never," Phyllis and Brenda said simultaneously. Everyone laughed and Brenda was happy to see how Patrick's pep talk put the light back into Molly's eyes.

"I'm a little bit worried that maybe William knew what

was going on." Phyllis looked at her brother with troubled eyes. "Did he know what his wife was up to?"

"Lady Pendleton didn't love anyone and that included William. He had no idea what was going on. From everything I've heard, he is a fine upstanding man, well respected and well known now that he is out from under her control. You will have a happy life with a very good man, Phyllis. I can't tell you how happy I am for you."

CHAPTER NINE

CLOSURE

When Brenda left the hospital, she walked to Blossoms. She wanted to talk with Jenny about the strange switch of partners that had occurred between her, Molly, Bryce and Pete. Something still nagged at her that the whole situation was somehow as false as Pete Graham's life had been.

Jenny Rivers smiled at Brenda as she finished a transaction with a customer. "I'll be right back in, Brenda. I'm going to help load these poinsettias into her car."

Brenda walked around the shop admiring more of the flowers, and especially the blooming Christmas cactus plants. Jenny had put her artistic touch into the shop's festive ambiance. She heard the voices of two employees in the back room creating arrangements for customers.

Jenny came back in brushing snow from her hair and shoulders.

"A huge mound of snow landed on my head when I walked under the edge of the canopy at the front door," she said, laughing. "I know it's not melting out there but for some reason a hunk of it just dropped down on me as I came back in." Her eyes twinkled like the nearby lights on the tree in the window display. "I got the order in this morning for yours and Phyllis's wedding flowers. What else can I get you?"

"I just need a few minutes of your time. Can we talk privately?"

Jenny told one of the workers to listen for the bell and take care of customers for a few minutes. Jenny and Brenda walked to the side area of the shop where two bistro tables and chairs were. In the corner, hot coffee brewed. Jenny poured two cups and they sat down.

"I haven't had a chance to talk to you about you and Bryce breaking up. I really feel bad about it all. Was that his idea or Pete's that the four of you mix up like that?"

"It certainly wasn't Bryce's idea, though Pete sent that message around town. It was all Pete's idea. You know, Brenda, Molly told me he brought it up right after she suggested she move in with him and said that they should start thinking about marriage. I guess he isn't all that interested in marriage and he thought this would take care of his problem." Jenny sipped her coffee. "I heard the news about Patrick Lindsey being found. I haven't heard many details but I can only imagine how happy Phyllis and Molly are about it. Just think, he disappeared five years ago and is suddenly back in Sweetfern Harbor!"

Brenda became aware that Molly had not spoken to Jenny and nor had her father given her information of the arrests yet. She would have to fill her in. "He was found right here in town. Someone kidnapped him and held him hostage for the entire five years."

Jenny opened her mouth wide to speak and then closed it. She stirred her coffee and took a drink, trying to digest this piece of news. "He disappeared just after he won that lawsuit against Lady Pendleton. Did she have anything to do with it?"

Brenda nodded her head and then said, "Don't spread this around, but I can tell you she was involved...but it's much deeper than that. I think you'd better talk with your father. If he hasn't given you details yet, he has a reason. You will be shocked at how everything unfolded."

Jenny immediately pulled out her mobile phone and called Mac. Brenda smiled to herself. She should have known Jenny Rivers wouldn't wait another minute to find out what happened. She watched her future daughter-in-law as she listened to the detective. When the call ended, she sat back down without a word. She rested her elbows on the table and rested her forehead in her hands. When she looked up, she finally spoke.

"I can't believe such a thing, Brenda. Never in my wildest imagination would I have thought Edward and Pete had anything to do with his disappearance. How horrible to think Patrick has been in that dungeon-like place all these years. My dad didn't tell me exactly who found him." Her eyes questioned Brenda.

"I found him." She went on to tell Jenny how it had happened.

"I'm sure he is more than thankful for you, Brenda. He was very lucky that you were on the case. I really admire you for how you stick to things to the end."

Brenda smiled. "I just can't let a case go unsolved if I can help it. Phyllis had only one gift request and it was that Patrick would be here to see her and William marry on Christmas Eve. She got her wish and that is my thanks. It's all I need."

"I must see Molly very soon. She must be devastated."

"She is upset, but I'm sure with support she will be fine."

"Aren't you two supposed to be working?" Bryce walked toward them. He looked at Jenny and Brenda could tell his mood was uncharacteristically serious. "Jenny, I don't know how you feel about that crazy idea Pete Graham came up with, but I don't like it at all. I mean, Molly is a nice girl, but I told her I can't do it. You mean everything to me. I want to get back with you the way we were. What do you think?"

Jenny jumped up and hugged him tight. "I love only you, Bryce. I didn't like the idea either. I went along with it in the hopes it would be temporary. Did you know about Pete?" She caught herself. "Of course you do. I sometimes forget you are in the middle of crime like my father is."

"I have to say it is still hard to process what he did. He was living a complete lie the whole time. I would never have believed he deceived Molly most of all."

They were wrapped in each other's arms, discussing how they felt about Pete's idea of switching partners and admitted each felt it was bizarre from the beginning. Brenda was ready to excuse herself and leave the two alone when Bryce stepped back and apologized to her for the way he had treated Jenny.

"I'm meeting with Mac in half an hour. I owe Tim an apology too. Right now, I have a more important question for you, Jenny. Do you forgive me for treating you like I did?"

"I forgive you. We all got caught up in Pete's scheme."

"In that case, I have one more question to ask you." He told Jenny to sit back down. He got down on one knee and took a small box out of his pocket. When Bryce opened it, a small ring glittered beautifully under the lights of the shop. He looked up at her with hope and love in his eyes. "Jenny Rivers, will you marry me?"

"Yes," she said. He slipped the ring onto her finger. Brenda clapped in appreciation as the two kissed to seal their engagement. Jenny's employees had come out of the back room and cheered as well.

"I really do have to go, but not before offering my congratulations to both of you." She kissed Jenny and then Bryce on the cheek and waved to them over her shoulder as she exited.

The snow had stopped. Carolers sang on corners and when she passed the pet store a family of six puppies frolicked in the window. Their mother watched from the corner of the display. Brenda stopped at the bridal shop next and caught the owner just before she closed. She was told her bridal gown would be ready for the final fitting the next day.

When she reached the end of her driveway, Brenda took time to gaze at the Queen Anne mansion that was hers. Every window held a white candle with a bulb that flickered like a real flame. From each windowsill hung a delicate green wreath. The largest Christmas tree was decorated and on full exhibition with lights and sparkling ornaments in the front window of the sitting room. Two more trees lit up the front windows at the end of each passageway of the bed and breakfast. Soft white and red lights looped around the row of low evergreen bushes that lined the front of the building.

"Everything is perfect," Brenda breathed in happiness.

She heard a car's tires crunching on the top layer of crusted snow. Mac stopped his car and got out and joined her.

"I'm ready for some hot chocolate," he said. "Do you want a ride on up to the house?"

Brenda shivered. She felt the warmth from the car heater through the open door. "I'll take you up on both ideas. It's cold out here." They got into the car. "This feels good," Brenda said.

Inside the bed and breakfast, they went into the kitchen. It was past dinner time so everyone was gone from the area until the next day. The kitchen sparkled. Brenda put the teakettle on the stove and they stood together looking out at the backyard. The yard light towered over the wintery scene. When the kettle whistled, Brenda took two cups and some cocoa from the cabinet. She prepared the hot chocolate while Mac retrieved miniature marshmallows. They sat at the wooden table for four in the kitchen corner and sipped the hot beverage. Brenda offered him oatmeal raisin cookies and they enjoyed the refreshments in companionable silence.

"I talked with William about how much he knew about his wife's deeds. He told me he had no idea at all what she was doing. It was only when he started cleaning out to get ready for Phyllis to move in that he found several manila envelopes of questionable paperwork that had belonged to Lady Pendleton. He was shocked to hear what she had been doing. He knew about her rent shenanigans and more than once told her he thought it was unfair. He had no idea she did that based on their private tax returns."

"Patrick assured Phyllis that William never had any part in any of it," Brenda said. "When he discovered what was going on he was shocked at first but said that he really shouldn't have been surprised. I'm so glad Patrick is alive. And glad that those two were caught. Who knows how long Patrick would have survived down in that terrible place?"

"It's too bad Lady Pendleton didn't live long enough to go to trial," Mac said. Brenda had to agree. "Let's go into the sitting room and enjoy that fireplace and splendid tree," he said.

They refilled their cups and moved to the fireplace. The logs were becoming embers and Mac replenished the wood. They sat close on the loveseat in front of the soon roaring fire. They were content with one another and with listening to the crackling logs.

"Just think, Brenda, in a short time we'll be able to do this every evening."

"Don't forget we'll both be working and may not have leisure time like this. You'll be called out on some crime and I'll be dealing with a guest who demands something no matter the hour."

His soft chuckle soothed her. "Well, we can dream, can't we?"

"I'm good at doing that."

CHAPTER TEN

CHRISTMAS EVE

*J*n two days Brenda would marry Mac Rivers. Her wedding dress fit perfectly and hung in her closet waiting for her to put it on. The entire staff seemed to be running everywhere. Instead of preparing for bed and breakfast guests they all prepared for the double wedding. The double wedding caught everyone up in the spirit of celebration. The chef directed her helpers to follow her recipes exactly. Sweet Treats added two more employees for the occasion to prepare delicacies for the wedding reception.

Blossoms went all out, checking every flower that came in for the big day. Jenny visited the Congregational Church several times to measure and to detail the arrangement plans for each flower.

Molly Lindsey carried in three large coffee urns through

the back door of the bed and breakfast. The chef thanked her and they placed them in the extra pantry off the kitchen.

"I have the specialty coffee still in my car," Molly said.

"Michael," the chef called, "you go out and bring in the coffee for Molly." The young man brought the two large bags in and asked what else needed to be done. "Count the folding chairs and scrub the two long tables. We'll need them for the reception. Brenda doesn't want the furniture rearranged any more than we have to. I think she wants it to look like a place to live in and not a hall of some kind."

Brenda met Phyllis in the second floor hallway. "I have no idea what to do," Brenda said. "Every time I start to help out someone shoos me away. What are you doing?"

"Nothing," Phyllis said with a small smile. "They won't let me do anything either."

"In that case, let's just leave them and go downtown. Are you finished with your Christmas shopping?"

Phyllis said she wasn't, and so the two women left the work to those who insisted on doing it. "I need to find something really special for Patrick. He's the only one on my list that I haven't bought for."

They window-shopped for a while. At the pet store they stopped and commented on the puppies. Brenda noticed that two more had found new homes for Christmas.

"They are so cute," Brenda said. "Why don't you get one for Patrick? Does he like animals?"

"He loves animals, especially dogs. He had two dogs while he was growing up and they were inseparable." The more Phyllis thought about it, the more she liked the idea. "I'll ask the shop owner if he can pick it up a few days after Christmas. He'll have his own place by that time."

They went inside and an agreement was made that Patrick could pick up the black and white puppy after Christmas. Once outside, Phyllis stopped. "Let's go back in and get one more."

When Brenda asked who the second one was for, Phyllis said, "I remember my father bought two for Patrick long ago. The reason was so one would have the company of the other when Patrick was in school all day long. I think he really meant our mother or he wouldn't have to entertain one dog when Patrick wasn't home." She smiled at the memory.

After purchasing the golden-brown one as a companion for the first one, they walked to Morning Sun Coffee. Molly parked her car and got out as they neared the shop.

"It looks like you two are free as birds," she said merrily. "Come on in for something hot to drink."

Both ordered lattés and enjoyed drinking them as they observed everyone shopping from the window. Some carried large parcels and others were still looking at windows trying to decide.

"I hate to see my father leave for Michigan again. He's been here since Thanksgiving and we've grown closer." Brenda really wanted her father to relocate to Sweetfern Harbor.

"Maybe he's waiting for you to ask him to move here."

"I hadn't thought of that, but maybe you're right. I'll talk with him tonight."

The rest of the day was leisurely but moved slower for Brenda than she wanted. She was accustomed to going hard all day long. She toyed with the idea of asking Mac if there were any unsolved cases she could look at and decided against it. Mac may be at home getting ready for their celebration. She went into her office and looked at bookings for New Year's and after. Allie had booked the entire month of January, beginning the second week. The exceptions were a few nights here and there.

That evening after dinner when everyone returned to their own homes, Brenda invited the few employees still there into the sitting room.

"Everything is so beautiful. All of you did a great job making this place shine for Christmas. I want you to slow down the next day or two. I can't think of anything that hasn't been done for the weddings already. It's a good time to relax and enjoy the season."

"I think everything is about ready," Allie said. "Of course, there will be last minute things the day of your weddings but things are shaping up. Can you believe you'll be married in less than two days?"

"I can't believe I'm lucky enough to find someone like Mac Rivers."

They enjoyed hot beverages in front of the stone fireplace and told stories of Christmases past. Allie excused herself and reminded Brenda she wouldn't be in until close to noon. She promised her mother she'd help with the baking at Sweet Treats. The rest took their cups to the kitchen and told everyone goodnight. Brenda and Phyllis were the only two left.

"I hope we don't have insomnia the next two nights," Phyllis said.

"Maybe a hot cup of tea will help us sleep tonight." Brenda gathered the rest of the remnants of the get-together and they washed and put everything away in the kitchen. Once upstairs, Brenda handed Phyllis a hot cup of lemon verbena tea and they parted for the night. Halfway through the beverage, Brenda's eyes grew heavy and she got ready for bed. That night she slept soundly.

The evening before Christmas Eve, Mac and William came by to pick up Brenda and Phyllis. They were to meet one last time with Reverend Walker at the church.

"We'll all go out and eat someplace afterwards, so dress up," Mac said. "William, this is our last night as bachelors. Maybe you and I should go celebrate."

"No one is going to celebrate too much tonight," Brenda said. "Both of you need to be in top form for tomorrow."

They all bantered back and forth but grew solemn when Mac rang the doorbell to the parsonage. Reverend Walker welcomed them inside and then they went to the church. He showed them where they were to stand and the general procedure of the ceremonies.

"Let your attendants know which side you will be on," he said to the women.

"We have the same bridesmaids," Brenda said.

The pastor thought for a few seconds. "Then tell them to separate on either side so the four of you will be centered."

Once finished, they walked outside to find light snowflakes coming down. William commented on the more than usual snow in recent days. Phyllis said she was happy they were going to have a white Christmas. Then they drove to the outskirts of Sweetfern Harbor and pulled into a restaurant that overlooked the ocean. The elevator was glassed in and they had a view of the beautiful snow-covered scenery until they reached the top. Mac and William had reserved the dining room for the four of them so they could celebrate in style. The women understood why Mac told them to dress up. Everything was elegant.

By the time they returned to the bed and breakfast that night, only the candles in the windows lit the place. Allie or perhaps the chef had left the foyer light on. William accompanied Phyllis to her apartment and Mac stepped inside with Brenda. He leaned down and kissed her. Without words, but with a huge smile, he caressed her hand before he turned and left for the night.

The next morning, Brenda awoke to soft carols coming from downstairs. There were no guests left at the bed and breakfast and she presumed her employees were in the Christmas spirit. When she came down, carolers stood in the foyer and broke into louder singing as she came down. They were all invited to the dining room for hot drinks and a light breakfast. When they left, Brenda told the few employees there to go home and enjoy Christmas Eve with their families.

"We'll celebrate tomorrow at our house," said one. The young girl was in her early twenties and had two children. "My kids don't open presents until Christmas morning anyway."

Everyone else had similar comments. The chef told her group to let Phyllis and Brenda do whatever they wanted today.

"If they want to pitch in, stand back and let them. They'll need to keep busy." Chef Morgan didn't miss the fact that just because they were going to be older brides didn't mean they weren't a little nervous.

By early afternoon, tables were set up and Brenda helped set things on the buffet and the sliders were set for hot dishes. The dining room was perfect. Phyllis was busy in the sitting room directing helpers to shift the furniture back a little to make walking room for guests later that night. The day passed quickly and it was time to get ready for the weddings.

Jenny, Hope, Molly and Allie went upstairs to an extra guest room where they would get ready for their parts in the wedding. Once dressed, Hope and Molly assisted Phyllis and Jenny and Allie helped Brenda get ready. When they all met in the hallway, the bridesmaids exclaimed over and over at how beautiful they looked. Their dresses fit perfectly and matched the Christmas theme nicely. Both brides beamed as they came downstairs. They were met with someone dressed as an old fashioned footman. He bowed to them all and told them their carriages waited for them.

All gasped with surprise when they saw three carriages lined up in front of Sheffield Bed and Breakfast.

"This looks like something Mac and William would think of," Brenda said to Phyllis.

"Without a doubt. Let's go, Cinderella," she said.

As they drew closer to the church, Sweetfern Harbor was alive with people along the street waving to them. When they arrived, the women were escorted into the side vestibule to give everyone time to settle in for the wedding. Jenny walked down the aisle first, to the beautiful sounds of the high school choir and the church organ. She was followed by Allie. They met the groomsmen and stood on the left side. Hope and Molly did the same and stood on the right side. Brenda was first to walk down the aisle on the arm of her father. Tim Sheffield beamed and whispered to his daughter how beautiful she looked. Brenda's heart was beating fast. She felt beautiful and blessed and everything looked perfect.

Phyllis, on the arm of her brother Patrick, followed her. Both met their husbands-to-be and fought to hold back tears of happiness.

The pink and red poinsettias that lined the front of the church blended with the festive greenery. On the altar was a huge bouquet of calla lilies, Phyllis's favorite flower. Brenda had asked for poinsettias, her favorite Christmas flower. In the middle of the bouquets was a candelabrum with candles that cascaded down in a sweeping motion. The ornate vase of calla lilies was on one side of it and the largest poinsettia Brenda had ever seen was on the other side. Jenny had outdone herself.

Brenda and Mac exchanged vows first and then Phyllis and William. Both of the couples kissed their mates and turned around to be introduced as Mr. and Mrs. Rivers, and Mr. and Mrs. Pendleton. Everyone applauded and as they walked back down the aisle, smiles spread across the congregation. Brenda looked up at Mac and thought how handsome he was. He looked at her and thought, how lucky could he get? She was beautiful in his mind and in truth, she was.

The carriages waited to take them to Sheffield Bed and Breakfast for the reception. The bridesmaids and groomsmen piled into the eight-seated carriage and followed. At the bed and breakfast, the entire structure was lit up. Christmas tree lights blazed and once inside they were all met with perfection in the way the bed and breakfast was set up. Every detail had been attended to. The wedding couples were escorted into the dining room. Brenda couldn't have imagined how it was transformed into this beauty, even though she had initially helped set things up just that morning. She held onto Mac and felt herself filled with happiness.

The guests buzzed happily among themselves and congratulated the newlyweds. Next to the shared wedding cake were wrapped Christmas gifts. After the cake was cut, Mac handed Brenda a small gift.

"This is something that you should have." His eyes twinkled, teasing her to open it.

When she unwrapped the gift, she pulled out something wrapped in red tissue paper that felt hard. It was a police badge with her name on it. She looked up at Mac. "You win," she said, laughing.

"You deserve to be on the police force and so you need an official badge."

"Remember that I'm not going to give up my position right here. But thank you. I will look quite official now." She kissed Mac. "Now open yours." She handed him one of her own.

Mac picked up the narrow rectangular box and opened it. Inside were carving tools. On the handles were the engraved words, *Pfeil Tools, Swiss Made*. Brenda remembered how much he liked to whittle and now he could go further with his hobby. He thanked her and they kissed. Everyone applauded again and Chef Morgan and her helpers came out and set hot food on the buffet and down the middle of the table. Individual cake plates were filled and placed on the buffet for everyone to help themselves.

Brenda had never been so happy in her life. She had the husband of her dreams and a town that had become her family. She looked across the room at her father, who beamed happily at her. The only thing missing was her mother, she thought. She felt for the pearl necklace at her throat and smiled. Her mother was there, too. Tim nodded in appreciation.

Tim Sheffield found his way to his daughter and new son-in-law. They had a place next to them for him to sit down. Jenny joined them and Phyllis, William and Patrick sat across the table from them. Tim whispered to Brenda he had some news for her that he hoped would make her happy.

CHAPTER ELEVEN

MORE SURPRISES

*M*ost eyes followed father and daughter as they spoke. Mac noticed the confidential air between them.

"No whispering at the table," Mac teased.

Tim looked at Brenda. She told him to let everyone hear it if he wanted to. He agreed and stood up.

"I am happy for my daughter and for Mac." He turned to Phyllis and congratulated her and William. "I have some news I'd like to share with all of you. My home in Michigan gets quite lonely at times. I'm a retired man now who tends to wander around looking for things to do. Since I've been in Sweetfern Harbor, I am astonished at how much goes on in this little town. If my daughter, and all of you, will have me, I've decided to make my home right here in this village. I want to become a greater part of her life and of yours."

Again everyone applauded and murmurs and shouts of welcome came from the guests. Brenda couldn't keep her tears at bay this time. She stood up and hugged her father. "I love you, Dad. It is what I hoped for. You can stay right here for as long as you want to."

Tim shook his head. "I've found a small cottage that fits me well. You have your business here and I've been taking up one of your rooms meant for paying guests. Now you have a husband to think about. The two of you need your privacy without me hanging around. I'll be just a few blocks from you. William has sold one of his rental properties to me." He turned to William who smiled and told Tim welcome to Sweetfern Harbor. William winked at Brenda as if to apologize for keeping this small secret from her.

Patrick stood up and toasted his sister and William. "This is one of the happiest days of my life," he said. "I toast my loving sister and her husband William Pendleton. May you enjoy long and happy lives together."

Then he turned to Brenda and Mac. "Congratulations to the woman who saved my life and to the man she so deserves. I wish only the best for both of you."

Everyone clapped and cheered. Patrick received several

pats on his back and many told him how happy they were that he was safe and sound.

This was a night of celebrations. Brenda leaned toward Mac. "There can't be anything else that happens on a night like this. What a perfect night."

"I think we've had all the surprises we can handle." Mac leaned closer to Brenda.

Someone gave a signal for silence. Brenda and Mac looked at each other and laughed. "I guess we may have been wrong," he said.

William and Phyllis stood up. She held a large envelope in her hand and beamed at her good friends.

"Phyllis is holding something we wanted to give to you, Brenda, and to Mac of course, now that you have made her an honest woman." Everyone laughed and waited to see what was in the envelope.

Phyllis handed it to Brenda. When she read the document, she gasped and looked at the couple and back to the words.

"They've paid off the Sheffield Bed and Breakfast mortgage," she said.

Mac took it and read it. "She's right. It is legally documented right here."

Brenda pushed her chair back and grabbed Phyllis, tears

in her eyes. "Thank you so much, Phyllis. And thank you too, William. This means more than you can imagine. Uncle Randolph would be so happy that it is free and clear now to continue for him."

Tim Sheffield clapped the loudest and his face radiated with love for his daughter and gratefulness for her friends. "Randolph would be happy for sure, Brenda."

Once dinner was over and everyone had eaten enough cake and desserts to last them through Christmas, people began to mingle with one another in small groups. Brenda joined Phyllis and Patrick just as she handed him a Christmas card.

"I don't have your gift with me right now, but it's, or rather, *they're* waiting for you downtown." Phyllis waited for him to read her card. He looked at her in surprise and curiosity.

"You are giving me dogs?" he said. Phyllis hesitated at first thinking he didn't like the idea. "I'm just kidding with that tone, Phyllis. You don't know how happy this makes me. I see you are following dad's directive to get two dogs. I hope I can keep them in the apartment. I'm not sure William will approve pets there."

Phyllis looked smug. "Don't worry. He doesn't object. He has a few houses to show you after we get back from our honeymoon. That is, if you plan to stay around here and would like a home of your own."

"I plan to stay right here. The new lawyer coming to town has already offered me a job in the law office downstairs from the apartment. I have plans to complete a degree in law. If I'm getting dogs, maybe a house would be better. I could fence it in and they could have room to run."

Phyllis told him the two houses William had in mind were already fenced. Brenda stepped forward and told Patrick how happy she was that he planned to stay around town. She left them and continued around the room to greet everyone. She saw Molly Lindsey quietly drinking a cold drink by herself.

"I want to thank you for everything you did for my wedding, Molly."

"You are more than welcome, Brenda. The ceremonies were beautiful." Brenda waited, knowing she wanted to say more. "I really miss Pete. I guess I mean I miss the Pete I thought he was. It was such a shock to me and I'm finding it hard to recover."

"I understand that, Molly. It will take time. In the meantime, you are always welcome to vent to me."

Molly smiled. "Here I am spoiling your happiest night."

Brenda patted her on the arm and assured her nothing could spoil this Christmas Eve. "Your mother was the first person to welcome me here. We've become very good friends, which means that you are my daughter, too."

Molly hugged her and told her thank you. Brenda knew that somehow everything would work out for Molly Lindsey.

Carolers began to sing again. The high school choir had moved from the church to the bed and breakfast to continue singing for the couples. Mac whispered in the ear of the choir director. He nodded and instructed his choir.

"This next song is specifically for the newlyweds." He turned to his choir and they sang "I'll Be Home for Christmas."

This time it was hard for anyone to hold back moisture from forming in their eyes. Mac pulled Brenda closer. "We have a flight to catch tomorrow morning. Do you think we should head for the hotel in New York any time soon?"

Brenda glanced at the crystal clock on the mantle as she swayed in his arms. It read eleven o'clock. "I think we should. I'll get out of this wedding dress and be right back down." Jenny was nearby. She gathered Hope, Allie and Molly and all went upstairs with Phyllis and Brenda.

"Don't worry about these gowns," Jenny said as they helped Brenda out of her dress. "We'll take care of everything." She kissed Brenda and told her welcome to the family. Brenda hugged her back.

Everyone stayed upstairs while Brenda went back down.

Mac waited for her at the bottom of the stairs. Guests gathered around. Phyllis and the bridesmaids watched from the top of the stairs. Mac took Brenda's hand and stopped her under the mistletoe at the front door. He kissed her and then helped her with her coat. Everyone cheered again and stood back for Phyllis and William to take their places under the mistletoe, too.

Outside, Tim hugged his daughter. He pulled back with mist in his eyes. "These are tears of joy, Brenda. I love you." She returned the sentiments before getting into the waiting limo. Jenny hugged her father and told him how happy she was for him and Brenda.

"Have a great time in Italy," she said. "Don't forget to come back. We need both of you."

"We'll be back, but I won't give you a specific date. Just in case we get too caught up with the Italian way of life," Mac joked.

Molly and Patrick walked with Phyllis and William to their limo. Everyone hugged and Molly and Patrick welcomed William to their family. Phyllis and William were eager to head off to the airport to fly to sunny beaches and cobalt blue waters.

Before the limos left, all four leaned out and wished everyone a Merry Christmas and a Happy New Year. The guests cheered from the porch of the bed and breakfast as they drove off. The driver asked them if they would like to listen to Christmas music. They opted for classical Christmas tunes with no words.

It felt good to Brenda and Mac to have ten days ahead with each other, far away from business and crime-solving. There would be no thinking about upcoming trials for two men once thought to be pillars of Sweetfern Harbor, and good friends. The Italian landscapes waited for them to explore and free their minds.

"I doubt I'll ever be happier than I am right now," Brenda said.

"I'm hoping to take care of that and give you happier ones in our future together."

Brenda snuggled closer to Mac. Christmas lights glittered down Main Street. Shops were closed but animations in various windows caught their attention. It appeared they were leaving their own private fairyland.

They took it all in as they listened to Tchaikovsky's Dance of the Sugar Plum Fairy send them off into the blissful peace of their waiting honeymoons.

ABOUT THE AUTHOR

Wendy Meadows is an emerging author of cozy mysteries. She lives in "The Granite State" with her husband, two sons, two cats and lovable Labradoodle.

When she isn't working on her stories she likes to tend to her flower garden, relax with adult coloring and play video games with her family.

Get in Touch with Wendy

www.wendymeadows.com

wendy@wendymeadows.com

CHOCOLATE COZY MYSTERY SERIES

Cream of Sweet

Itsy-Bitsy Murder

Fudgement Day

A's in the Hole

ALASKA COZY MYSTERY SERIES

The Snowman Killer

Deep in the Snow

Snow Happens

Snow is not the Time

Made in the USA
Middletown, DE
25 July 2021

44794461R00080